DOCTOR WHO AND
THE PYRAMIDS OF MARS

DOCTOR WHO
AND THE
PYRAMIDS OF MARS

Based on the BBC television serial *Pyramids of Mars*
by Stephen Harris by arrangement with the British
Broadcasting Corporation

TERRANCE DICKS

A TARGET BOOK
published by
the Paperback Division of
W. H. ALLEN & Co. Ltd

A Target Book
Published in 1976
by the Paperback Division of W. H. Allen & Co. Ltd
A Howard & Wyndham Company
44 Hill Street, London W1X 8LB

Second impression 1979

Printed in Great Britain by
Richard Clay (The Chaucer Press), Ltd., Bungay, Suffolk
ISBN 0 426 11666 6

Contents

Prologue

The Legend of the Osirians

In a galaxy unimaginably distant from ours, on a planet called Phaester Osiris, there arose a race so powerful that they became like gods.

As well as mastering technology and science, the Osirians developed powers of pure thought, bending the physical world to their will by the strength of their minds alone.

As they grew in power, so they grew in wisdom—all but one. His name was Sutekh and he was great among the Osirians. But greater still was his brother Horus, whom all Osirians called leader. All but Sutekh, who hated Horus and was jealous of him.

The Osirians spread throughout the galaxies of the cosmos. They ruled many worlds, and were often worshipped as gods. But Sutekh stayed on Phaester Osiris, their home planet, working to develop his powers so that he might one day overthrow his brother Horus.

The Osirians were a long-lived race. Sutekh worked and studied for thousands of years, until his powers were truly awe-inspiring. But his mind was full of jealousy and hatred, and in time this turned to madness. Over-mastered by his own fears, Sutekh became convinced that not only the other Osirians, but *all* sentient life was his mortal enemy. Not just the more intelligent life-forms, but animals, reptiles, insects, plants ... Sutekh hated them all. He feared that someday, somewhere there might evolve a life-form powerful enough to destroy him.

An insane ambition formed in Sutekh's twisted mind. He would range through the galaxies and destroy *all* life, until only he remained as unchallenged ruler. He became Sutekh the Destroyer—and he began by destroying his own planet.

Leaving the shattered desolation of Phaester Osiris behind him, Sutekh blazed a trail of havoc across the cosmos, wrecking and smashing world after world with his titanic powers. Soon news of his madness reached fellow Osirians. Led by Horus, they began the search for Sutekh, determined to destroy him.

Tracking him by his trail of destruction, they hunted him across the cosmos. At last Sutekh took refuge on an obscure planet called Earth, and here, finally, his fellow Osirians found him.

The battle was long and fierce, for Sutekh was a formidable opponent. Seven hundred and forty Osirians came to Earth to combine against him, before he was finally defeated and made captive, in a land called Egypt.

They brought him before his brother Horus for judgement. Many urged that all the Osirians should link their minds and blast Sutekh from existence. But Horus would not agree. To kill Sutekh would mean that they too were destroyers. Horus decreed that Sutekh should not die but should be made eternally captive. A pyramid was built to become his prison. And since more than walls of stone were needed to imprison such a being as Sutekh, he was locked in the grip of a mighty forcefield, paralysed and utterly helpless.

For even greater safety, the control-point of this forcefield was placed not on Earth, but on one of the other planets circling its sun. On Earth, a secret cult of Egyptian priests was set up, to guard the Pyramid.

Satisfied that Sutekh was for ever bound, Horus and the other Osirians went on their way. What became of the Osirians no one can say. They vanished from our cosmos and were seen no more. On Earth they left behind them legends of the all-powerful gods who fought wars among themselves.

Deep inside the Pyramid, Sutekh lived on. For thousands upon thousands of years he endured his long captivity. Bound by the forcefield of Horus, scarcely able to move a muscle, only his twisted brain was active. It planned and plotted without cease, waiting for the day of his escape. For Horus would not leave even Sutekh quite without hope. He had told him that escape *was* possible, though the difficulties and obstacles were so great as to be almost insurmountable.

The mighty civilisation of Egypt rose and fell. Other civilisations and Empires took its place. Sutekh and Horus and the Osirians were remembered only as a legend. Still Sutekh waited in his hidden Pyramid. Until one day ...

I

The Terror is Unleashed

In a hidden valley, shimmering in the blazing heat of the Egyptian sun, two men stood gazing at the squat black shape of a Pyramid. One was an Egyptian in tattered, striped robes and red fez. The other was tall and thin, with a keen, scholarly face. Despite the heat, he wore a white tropical suit, with stiff collar and public school tie. The year was 1911, and Englishmen abroad were expected to maintain certain standards.

The Englishman was Professor Marcus Scarman and he was a dedicated Egyptologist. At this moment, his eyes were blazing with controlled excitement as he gazed on the greatest discovery of his career. A secret Pyramid of unfamiliar design, tucked away in a valley still unvisited by other Egyptologists. Here was a find to make him the envy of all his rivals. Rumours of the existence of a hidden Black Pyramid, centre of some secret native cult, had long been circulating in achaeological circles. Many had scoffed at them. But Marcus Scarman had passed long years tracking them down, spending many English sovereigns to buy information in the bazaars of Cairo. At long last he had found Ahmed, whose love of gold had finally overcome his fear. They had journeyed together into the desert for many days, and now they had arrived.

Near by, a gang of half-naked Egyptian labourers squatted patiently by the tethered camels. Marcus made a brief examination of the exterior of the Pyramid, then beckoned them over. 'There's a sealed entrance—here. Shouldn't take you long to get it open. Ahmed, go and fetch two lanterns.' The labourers began swinging their picks, and Marcus watched impatiently as they chipped away mortar and started lifting aside the heavy stone blocks. As soon as the space was big enough, he pushed them aside. 'All right, that'll do. Ahmed, tell them to wait here. You come with me.' Eagerly Marcus climbed through the gap, Ahmed following cautiously behind him.

They found themselves in a long stone-walled tunnel, going deep into the heart of the Pyramid. Marcus pressed eagerly ahead. The tunnel led into a huge echoing burial chamber. Marcus held up his lantern and looked around. The light flickered eerily off jewelled caskets and ornately decorated golden urns. 'Perfect,' he breathed. 'Absolutely perfect and quite untouched. The reliquaries are still sealed. Great Heavens, what a find! This tomb must date back to the first dynasty of the Pharaohs.'

Ahmed looked about nervously, sharing none of the Englishman's enthusiasm. In the dank, echoing darkness of the burial chamber, surrounded by mysterious shapes, he was overcome by the fear that he was blaspheming the ancient gods of his people. Surely there would be punishment ...

Too absorbed to notice his companion's lack of enthusiasm, Marcus moved through the chamber, till he reached the wall at its far end. The wall was hung with a jewel-encrusted tapestry of enormous value. Marcus stretched out a trembling hand and touched it reverently. 'How many thousands of years since the priests sealed the inner chamber, and draped this tapestry over the entrance?' he whispered to himself. It was obvious from the rich furnishings of the burial chamber that this had been the tomb of some great one of ancient times. But whose? Impatient to know the answer, Marcus reached out and carefully drew back the tapestry. Behind it was a wall built from blocks of stone. The mortar between them was old and crumbling—the wall would be easy to move away. As he studied it, Marcus became aware of something strange. In the centre of the wall a glowing red light had appeared. It actually seemed to come from deep *inside* the stone ... Marcus turned to the Egyptian. 'Ahmed! Your lantern, man. Quickly!'

Reluctantly Ahmed came forward, holding up his lantern. In the light of the two lanterns, the ruby-red glow burned even brighter.

Ahmed backed away. 'It is the Eye—the Eye of Horus!' he muttered in his own language. 'It is a warning. Do not cross the threshold of the gods or you will die!' Dropping his crowbar with a clatter, Ahmed turned and ran, back down the stone passage towards the daylight.

Marcus Scarman called after him angrily. 'Come back here, I need your help!'

All he heard in reply was the wailing voice of the Egyptian, echoing down the tunnel. 'If you cross the threshold of the gods you will die ...'

'Superstitious savage,' muttered Marcus. He looked back at the wall. The eerie red glow had faded. Determinedly he picked up Ahmed's crowbar. 'I've come

12

too far to turn back now ...' He jammed the crowbar into a crevice and began to heave. Mortar crumbled away beneath his onslaught. Marcus jammed the crowbar deeper. Groaning with effort he heaved again ...

There came a deep, hollow grinding sound, and a whole section of the wall swung away. Marcus stepped forward into the gap, and was immediately transfixed by a blaze of green light. He looked upwards. Above him there hovered an indescribably malignant face, a mask of pure evil. Marcus tried to scream but the sound was locked in his throat. Then came a sudden huge blast of sound, like a discord from some enormous organ. The wave of sound seemed to lift Marcus's body and hurl it to the ground. He lay sprawled out, limp and motionless, eyes closed and face a deathly grey.

Through the swirling chaos of the Space/Time Vortex, that strange continuum where Space and Time are one, there sped the incongruous shape of a square blue police box, light flashing on the top. Inside the police box, which was not a police box at all, was a vast ultra-modern control room, dominated by a many-sided centre console of complex instruments. A tall man was staring intently into the console's glowing central column. He had a mobile intelligent face crowned with a mop of curly brown hair. A battered, broad-brimmed hat was jammed on the back of his head, an extraordinarily long scarf trailed around his neck. His usually cheerful features were set in a frown of brooding intensity.

An inner door opened, and a slender, dark-haired girl came into the control room. She wore an attractive, old-fashioned dress. 'Look what I've found, Doctor.'

The Doctor glanced at her absentmindedly. 'Hello, Victoria.'

The girl, whose name was Sarah Jane Smith, looked at him indignantly. 'Hello *who*?'

The Doctor looked up, emerging from his abstraction. 'Oh, it's you, Sarah. Where did you get that dress?'

'I found it in the wardrobe. Why, don't you like it?'

The Doctor nodded vaguely. 'Oh yes, I always did. It belonged to Victoria. She travelled with me for a time.'

The Doctor smiled at the memory of Victoria, always so frightened, always trying so hard to be brave. Finally the strain had been too much for her and she'd left the TARDIS to return to Earth, though in a period much later than her own Victorian age.

Sarah looked at the Doctor thoughtfully. There was no doubt about it, the Doctor in his fourth incarnation was a distinctly more elusive character. Sarah suddenly realised how little she really knew about him. She knew he was a Time Lord, with the ability to travel through Space and Time in the strange craft he called the TARDIS—initials which stood for Time and Relative Dimensions in Space. She knew, because she'd seen it happen, that he had the power to transform his appearance, replacing a damaged body with what seemed to be a completely new one.

Sarah had first met the Doctor in his capacity of

Scientific Adviser to UNIT, the United Nations Intelligence Taskforce, that special organisation set up to protect Earth from attack from outer space. Brigadier Lethbridge-Stewart, head of UNIT's British Section, had known the Doctor for a very long time, and looked upon him as a valued colleague. Sarah had been the Doctor's companion on many adventures, both before and after his change of appearance. But she realised that the Doctor had had many lives and many companions, and that she had been involved in only a small proportion of his adventures.

The Doctor's usual mood was one of infectious high spirits. But very occasionally he would lapse into a kind of brooding thoughtfulness, when it was very difficult to get through to him. She tried to cheer him up. 'So the dress was Victoria's? Well, as long as it wasn't Albert's, I'll wear it.' The Doctor went on staring at the control column. 'Oh come on, Doctor,' said Sarah. 'That was worth a smile, surely? What's wrong? Aren't you glad to be going home?'

The Doctor looked up. 'Earth isn't my home, Sarah,' he said sadly. 'I'm a Time Lord, remember, not a human being ... I walk in eternity.'

'And what's that supposed to mean?'

'It means I've lived for something like—oh, seven hundred and fifty years, in your terms.'

'Soon be getting middle-aged,' said Sarah lightly.

Once again the Doctor ignored her little joke. 'What's more,' he went on, 'it's high time I found something better to do than run round after the Brigadier.'

Sarah smiled. So that was it. The Doctor still resented being summoned back to Earth by the Brigadier to deal with the Zygon invasion.* Sarah sympathised but she was determined not to encourage him in his sulk. 'If you're getting tired of being UNIT's Scientific Adviser, you can always ...'

A sudden terrific jolt shook the TARDIS, and Sarah was flung across the console. '... resign,' she gasped, completing her sentence. 'Doctor, what was that? What's happened?'

The Doctor was too busy to answer her. His hands flickered rapidly over the console as he fought to bring the TARDIS back under control. The TARDIS rocked and spun, and a deep thrumming noise filled the air, like a discord from some giant organ. Sarah lost her hold on the console and staggered across the control room. She fell in a heap in a corner and gazed muzzily upwards. There seemed to be a cloud of smoke. Was the TARDIS on fire?

A hideous face, malignant and somehow bestial, had formed in the smoke cloud and was glaring down at her. It seemed half human, half wolf or jackal. Sarah screamed ...

The apparition vanished, the organ noise stopped, the TARDIS settled down. Everything was back to normal. Sarah picked herself up and ran across to the Doctor. She grabbed his arm. 'Doctor, what *was* it?'

The Doctor was absorbed in his instruments. 'The relative continuum stabiliser failed. Odd—that's never happened before.'

'No, not the upset. I mean that *thing*!—and that noise?'

* See 'Doctor Who and the Loch Ness Monster'

He gave her a puzzled look. 'What thing? What noise?'

Sarah shuddered. 'It was like an organ ... and I saw this horrible face ... Just for a second, then it was gone.'

The Doctor looked at her. Indignantly, Sarah said, 'You don't believe me, do you?'

'My dear Sarah, nothing hostile can possibly enter the TARDIS. Unless ...' The Doctor broke off suddenly and returned to the console. 'Mental projection?' he muttered to himself. 'Mental projection of that force is beyond belief ... and yet—it could explain the stabiliser failure! Now let me see, it was at this end of the spectrum ...' The Doctor's hands once again began moving over the controls.

Sarah tugged him away from the console. 'No, Doctor. Please don't try and bring it back. Whatever that thing was, it was totally evil ...'

There was another, smaller jolt, and the central column stopped moving. 'We've arrived, Sarah. UNIT H.Q.!' The Doctor checked the instruments, operated the door control.

'Hang on a minute,' said Sarah hurriedly. 'I know we've landed somewhere. But are you sure ...'

She was too late. The Doctor was already outside. Sarah sighed and followed him.

They found themselves in a large, well-proportioned ground-floor room, with windows facing on to a garden. The TARDIS was in a corner surrounded by huge packing cases. The room looked like a miniature museum. All around stood various forms of Egyptiana —mummy cases, funeral urns, painted wooden chests.

Many were already on display and others simply scattered about. It was as though someone had brought home an enormous collection of Egyptian relics, but hadn't yet finished unpacking all of them. Sarah threw the Doctor an accusing look. 'UNIT H.Q.?'

The Doctor cleared his throat. 'Ah, well ... you see, we've arrived at the correct point in Space, but obviously not in Time. We've had a temporal reverse. Some vast energy-impulse has drawn the TARDIS off course.' The Doctor smiled, evidently quite satisfied by his own explanation.

Sarah looked around. 'Are you telling me this is UNIT H.Q., years before I knew it?'

The Doctor nodded. 'That's right.'

'But it's all so different. This isn't even the same house.'

'No, it isn't ...' Suddenly the Doctor smiled. 'Of course, this must be the Old Priory. The UNIT house was built on the same site.'

'So it was. The Old Priory burnt down, didn't it?'

The Doctor held up his hand for silence.

'What is it?'

'Atmosphere,' said the Doctor mysteriously. 'I sense alien vibrations. There's something very wrong here, Sarah ...'

A deep, discordant organ-note shattered the silence. Sarah looked fearfully at the Doctor. 'That's the noise I heard before. That thing that came into the TARDIS—it must be here, somewhere in this house ...'

2

The Mummy Awakes

In the organ room on the other side of the house, an immaculately dressed Egyptian called Ibrahim Namin sat at the keyboard. His thin brown fingers swept across the keys, filling the room with a crescendo of discordant sound. The room quivered and shook with the deep throbbing chords. They created an atmosphere of madness, of chaos in which all normal laws were suspended. The room was thick with a sense of ancient evil.

As he played, Namin glanced from time to time at an alcove just beyond the organ. In it stood an upright Mummy casket, richly decorated, flanked by four ceremonial urns. Namin's music was a kind of prayer, a tribute to his gods. He was the High Priest of the Cult of the Black Pyramid.

Namin had served the Cult all his life, like his ancestors before him. For thousands upon thousands of years the priests had served the high ones who built the Pyramid, carrying out the proper ceremonies, ensuring that the Black Pyramid in its secret valley remained inviolate. Then scholars from the West had come with their expeditions, prying into the ancient secrets. One day Namin heard the news he had always dreaded—an archaeological expedition was on its way to the Black Pyramid.

Namin and his fellow-priests had sped there at once.

The fleeing Ahmed and the terrified labourers had all been captured and killed instantly, their bodies buried in the desert. Then, in fear and trembling, Namin had entered the desecrated Pyramid, prepared to die for having failed his trust. To his terror and delight, one of the Great Ones had spoken to him. All was well. The Great Ones were not displeased—the opening of the Pyramid was a part of their plan. Namin had been given his orders. Now, in a strange land wearing strange clothes, he served the Great Ones as before. At first Namin had been very puzzled by these orders. In the Secret Writings of his cult it was laid down that the Pyramid must *never* be broken into, or the most terrible disaster would overwhelm the world.

But Sutekh, the Great One within the Pyramid, had told him the writings were mistaken. The Pyramid was a prison in which he had been cast by treachery, thousands of years ago. Now the time was approaching for his release. Soon Sutekh would return to rule the world. Ibrahim Namin and his fellow-priests would be exalted as they had been in ancient times, rulers of the people, and servants of the Great Ones.

Many and complicated were the tasks that had been laid upon Ibrahim Namin. He had to go to a hotel in Cairo, posing as the servant of Professor Scarman, and obtain the Professor's luggage. He had to hire work-men to make wooden crates, and porters to carry them to the Pyramid.

Inside the Pyramid, many sacred objects were packed by the hands of Ibrahim and his fellow priests.

All these crates had first to be taken to Cairo, then shipped to England. Strangest of all, Ibrahim Namin was ordered to accompany them to this house in England, guarding them most strictly all the while. Once in the house, he was to install himself and wait, allowing no one to enter or to touch the sacred relics.

All this Namin had done. But he was not too happy in England. Although Collins, the servant of the house, had accepted his letter of authority, it was clear that he was puzzled and suspicious. The brother of Professor Scarman had also been a source of trouble, protesting vigorously when barred from the house. A certain Doctor Warlock in the village had written a letter inquiring about Professor Scarman. Namin had ignored it. On his rare visits to the village, he was aware of a climate of hostility and suspicion. Surrounded by infidels and strangers, Namin pined for the burning deserts of his own country. He began to dream of the day when he would return as a great man, no longer priest of an obscure sect but king, a ruler of the world on behalf of the Great One. He hoped the time would not be long in coming ... Something disturbed his reverie. He looked up angrily. Through the clamour of his own playing, he could hear a knocking at the door.

In the corridor outside, an elderly man in the formal black clothes of an upper servant was hammering on the heavy wooden door. He had little hope that Namin would hear him over the noise of the organ, or would bother to answer if he did. But Collins had been in service all his life. Even though things at the Old Priory had changed so drastically, he still knew the proper way to behave in a gentleman's household.

Salvaging his conscience with another barrage of knocks, Collins flung open the door. Namin looked up angrily from the keyboard, still crashing out great discords on the organ.

Collins called, 'Excuse me, sir ...' but his quavery old voice was swallowed up by the noise.

Namin shouted, 'Get out. Get out of here!' He rose from the organ, and as the thundering discords died away, Namin stalked angrily towards the old servant. 'How dare you disturb me! Get out at once.'

Collins stood his ground. 'I'm sorry, sir. But the gentleman insisted.'

'Gentleman? What gentleman?'

'An old friend of Professor Scarman's, sir.'

Namin's black eyes blazed with fury. 'I ordered that no one was to be admitted, Collins. I told you no callers.'

A burly figure in country tweeds shouldered his way past Collins and into the room. 'Don't blame Collins, sir. I'm afraid it's a case of forced entry. Since you didn't answer my letter ...'

Namin glared angrily at the intruder. 'This is an outrage ...'

'Call it what you like. I've a few questions to put to you, and I'm not leaving till I've asked them.'

Namin looked thoughtfully at the ruddy-faced, balding figure in front of him. A typical English country gentleman, with all the unthinking arrogance of his kind. Clearly he wouldn't give up easily. Controlling his anger Namin said, 'All right, Collins, you may go.' Thankfully Collins scuttled away. Namin turned to his visitor. 'So! You have questions, have you? May I ask who you are?'

'My name's Warlock. Doctor Warlock. Live in the village. Marcus Scarman happens to be my oldest friend.'

Namin gave a curt nod. 'I am Ibrahim Namin. I——'

'I know your name,' interrupted Warlock brusquely. 'It's your business I'm concerned with. Called at the Lodge on my way up, had a word with Laurence. He tells me you've had the infernal impudence to bar him from this house.'

'I am acting on the direct orders of Professor Scarman.'

'Marcus Scarman ordered you to shut out his own brother? I don't believe it.'

Namin made a mighty effort to control himself. 'I have Professor Scarman's letter of authority. I have brought from Egypt all the relics discovered by the Professor on his recent expedition. My orders are to store them safely, and to allow no one admittance to the house until the Professor himself returns.' Namin's voice rose to an angry shout. 'And that is the end of the matter, Doctor Warlock!'

Warlock was quite unimpressed. 'Oh no it isn't, sir. Not by a long chalk!'

In the corridor outside, Collins listened to the angry voices, shaking his head in dismay. He was confused and frightened by all that had happened since Namin's arrival, but had thought it best to accept the orders in the letter. Now Warlock's visit was making him wonder if he'd done the right thing after all.

He turned to go, looking worriedly around the hall. Something caught his eye. The handle of a door on the far side of the hall was *moving*. Collins saw it turn, first one way and then the other, as someone tried to open the locked door ...

On the other side, the Doctor took his hand away from the door-knob. 'Why bother to lock all these internal doors?' he asked aggrievedly.

Sarah shrugged. 'Obviously this wing of the house isn't in use. It smells awfully musty.'

'More Mummy than musty,' said the Doctor cheerfully. The challenge of a new adventure had restored his usual good spirits. He produced a wire contraption from his pocket. 'French picklock. Never fails. Belonged to Marie Antoinette, charming lady, pity she lost her head poor thing ...'

Sarah grinned at the Doctor's flow of cheerful nonsense. Suddenly she tensed. From the other side of the door came the sound of a key turning in a lock. The Doctor took Sarah's arm and led her away.

Collins opened the door into the passage. It was empty. Puzzled he moved along to the Egyptian Room.

When Collins came in, the Doctor was leaning against a packing case, hands in his pocket, chatting to Sarah. 'A house like this would make an ideal headquarters for some semi-military organisation,' he was saying. 'This room could easily be converted into a laboratory ...'

Collins looked at the two intruders in astonishment. 'Who are you? How did you get in here?'

'We popped in through the window,' said the Doctor airily. 'I understood the property was for sale. I wanted to take a look.'

Collins was shaking his head shrewdly. 'You're not fooling me, sir. You came with Doctor Warlock, didn't you?'

'Did we?'

Collins gave a knowing nod. 'Asked you to scout round, didn't he, while he kept his nibs busy?' The old man's face became suddenly grave. 'Listen, sir, if you *are* a friend of Doctor Warlock's—tell him to watch out!'

'Watch out for what?' asked Sarah.

Collins turned to her. 'That Egyptian gentleman's got the temper of the devil, miss. No telling what he might do if he knew you'd been here, in the Egyptian room.'

The Doctor glanced round the cluttered room. 'A live Egyptian, eh? I suppose this is where he keeps his relatives?' The old man looked blankly at him. 'Relatives ... *Mummies* ...' said the Doctor hopefully. 'Oh, never mind.'

'It's no joke, sir,' said Collins sternly. 'Mr Namin's only been here a short while, but I can tell you, I wouldn't be staying myself only ... well I've worked for the Scarmans for a very long time. I keep hoping Mr Marcus will come back.'

As he talked the old man kept looking nervously over his shoulder.

'You're frightened,' said the Doctor suddenly. 'What are you afraid of?'

Collins lowered his voice. '*He* locked this wing. Ordered it all sealed off. He'd go stark, staring mad if he caught *me* in the Egyptian room, and as for you two ... Please go now, sir, for my sake.'

The Doctor looked thoughtfully at him. 'I see ... Well, if it's like that, perhaps we had better leave.'

He moved towards the door, but the old man caught his sleeve. 'Not that way, sir, he might see you. Go the way you came—through the window.'

Trapped by his own story, the Doctor glanced at Sarah, then turned back to the old man. 'As you wish,' he said gently.

They moved to the window. The Doctor opened it and started to climb out. Collins leaned closer to him and whispered, 'Remember to tell Doctor Warlock what I said, sir.'

'I'll remember, don't worry.' The Doctor helped Sarah through the window and Collins closed it behind them.

Old Collins watched the disappearance of the Doctor and Sarah with great relief. They'd seemed pleasant enough, but there would be the devil to pay if that Egyptian discovered they'd been in the house. Particularly in the Egyptian room, which was his particular obsession.

Collins looked round the room sadly, remembering the long hours Mr Marcus used to spend here, sorting through all his Egyptian stuff. Nasty old rubbish, Collins called it. But Mr Marcus was mad on it, had been ever since he was a child. From the very beginning he'd turned this room into a kind of museum, with all his treasures proudly displayed.

Collins looked gloomily at the pile of packing cases. Now there was a fresh batch of the stuff, cluttering up the house. No doubt Mr Marcus would want it all unpacked, the minute he got home.

Collins frowned at the sight of a tall blue box in the corner. He didn't remember seeing that one before. It had probably been delivered while he was in the village ... Crates had been arriving from Egypt for days now. Heaven knows how much more junk would turn up before Mr Marcus arrived to deal with it.

Muttering and grumbling to himself, Collins began shuffling around the room. He fished out an old rag and did a bit of defiant dusting. Whatever that Egyptian gentleman said, he wasn't going to neglect his duties. He dusted one of the newly-arrived Mummy cases, glaring at it disapprovingly. It wasn't the first Mummy they'd had in the house, of course. Mr Marcus had explained all about Mummies, but Collins still didn't care for them. As far as he was concerned, a dead body was a dead body and its place was in a cemetery, not in a gentleman's house.

Absorbed in his dusting and his grievances, old Collins didn't notice when the lid of one of the Mummy cases started to open. It opened further, then further, swinging fully back with a crash. Collins looked up in horror as a huge bandage-wrapped figure began stalking towards him ...

The Doctor and Sarah were moving through a dense shrubbery, which ran close to the side of the house. All around them was the beauty of an English country garden in summertime. The smooth green lawn, broken up with hedges and flower-beds, stretched away to the woods which surrounded the house. There was the hum of bees around a white-painted hive, the occasional chirrup of a bird. It was hard to reconcile this peaceful scene with the atmosphere of exotic horror in the room they had just left.

Sarah caught up with the Doctor and whispered, 'Where are we going?'

'I'm rather interested to see what this fearsome Egyptian looks like, aren't you?'

Sarah wasn't, but before she could say so, they heard angry voices from a near-by ground-floor window. One voice was gruff and very English, the other smooth and sibilant, with a marked foreign accent.

'Humbug!' roared the English voice. 'Utter humbug! That letter is a fabrication if ever I saw one.'

'You allege that it is forged?' hissed the foreign voice angrily.

'I do, sir, and I intend to prove it.'

'I warn you, Doctor Warlock, do not interfere!'

'Are you threatening me, sir?'

Intrigued by this very promising quarrel, the Doctor and Sarah edged closer to the window.

Inside the organ room, Warlock and Namin stood glaring at each other. Warlock was bristling like an angry bulldog, and Namin was quivering with rage. 'It is not *I* who threaten,' he whispered. 'There are ancient forces gathering in this place. Powers of ancient purpose, beyond the comprehension of mere unbelievers.'

'Powers of ancient balderdash!' said Warlock contemptuously. 'Let me warn you, Namin, unless you give me some honest answers, I'm going straight to the police.'

28

'To tell them what? That some suspicious foreigner is actually daring to live in Professor Scarman's house?'

Warlock's voice was calm and determined. 'To tell them that Professor Scarman has not been seen for weeks. To tell them that he left Cairo quite some time ago, and no one has seen him since. Oh yes, I've had inquiries made in Egypt ...'

A quavering scream, suddenly cut off, echoed through the room. 'What the devil ...' said Warlock. He ran from the room, heading in the direction of the sound. The Egyptian hesitated, then followed.

The window slid cautiously open, and the Doctor and Sarah started to climb in.

Doctor Warlock rushed into the Egyptian room, then stopped abruptly. The dead body of Collins lay on the floor, bulging eyes staring sightlessly at the ceiling. Horrified, Warlock knelt by the body, not noticing that a near-by Mummy case was quietly closing ...

Warlock looked up as Namin hurried into the room. 'The poor fellow's been strangled.'

There was no shock or horror on Namin's face, only a look of exaltation. His voice was triumphant. 'The gods have returned! I, Ibrahim Namin, servant of the true faith, rejoice in their power!'

'Fellow's cracked,' thought Warlock to himself. He stood up. 'We'd better get the police, the murderer can't have got far.'

Namin rounded on him. 'You blind pathetic fool! The servants of the all-powerful have arisen. When the temple is cleansed of all unbelievers, the high ones themselves will come among us. Thus it was written.'

More than ever convinced that he was dealing with a madman, Warlock spoke soothingly. 'Yes, I see, old chap. Still, I think the police ...' His voice tailed off. A small black automatic had appeared in Namin's hand.

Menacingly the Egyptian said, 'You should have listened when I told you to leave, Doctor Warlock. Now you have seen too much. You shall be the second unbeliever to die!' He levelled the gun at Warlock's heart.

The Doctor appeared silently in the doorway behind Namin. Just as the Egyptian pulled the trigger, the Doctor's scarf looped out over his head and shoulders, jerking backwards. The gun exploded, and Warlock staggered, clutching his shoulder.

The Doctor tried to get hold of the gun, but Namin was lithe and active, and seemed incredibly strong. He twisted the barrel of the automatic towards the Doctor's head, just as the Doctor gave him a shove that sent him flying across the room. Namin landed in the corner, the gun dropping from his hand. Quickly the Doctor and Sarah bustled the reeling Warlock from the room, slamming the door behind them.

Namin scrambled cat-like to his feet, picking up the gun. He seemed about to set off in pursuit, then suddenly stopped himself. The gun disappeared inside his coat, and Namin straightened his clothing and smoothed his hair. He moved to a near-by Mummy case and flung it open. Inside stood the huge bandage-wrapped figure of a Mummy. Namin raised his hand, and the ornate ruby ring on his finger glowed bright red. 'Arise!' he chanted. 'In the name of the High Ones, I command thee—arise!'

Slowly, the Mummy stepped from the case.

In the hall Sarah supported the wounded Warlock, while the Doctor dragged a heavy chest across the floor and jammed it against the door to the East Wing. 'That should hold him for a while. Right, come on!' They ran out of the house by the front door. Behind them the barricade began to shake under the impact of a powerful shove.

On the other side, Namin found the weight of the chest too much for him and stepped aside. He spoke to the towering form beside him. 'Open it,' he commanded. The Mummy stalked forward. It smashed open the barricaded door with ease, sending the heavy chest flying across the hall to crash against a distant wall.

Namin ran into the hall, the Mummy close behind him. 'This way!' ordered the Egyptian. Followed by his ghastly servant, he hurried across the hall and through the open front door.

The Doctor and Sarah were deep in the woods surrounding the house. They could have escaped with ease by now, but their pace was slowed by the wounded Warlock. The spreading bloodstain on his shoulder was widening steadily, despite Sarah's attempts to staunch it with a handkerchief, and his face was white. Suddenly he slid to the ground. 'No good,' he muttered, 'can't go further.'

The Doctor looked back. They were still quite close

to the house. 'I'm afraid you must,' he said urgently. 'We're sitting ducks out here in the open.'

Warlock shook his head. 'I ... can't ... Get to the Lodge ... just by main gates. Tell Laurence ... Scarman's brother. He lives there ...'

Warlock's head rolled back. He was unconscious.

The Doctor straightened up. 'He needs help badly. Sarah, you go on and find this Laurence.'

'What about you?'

'I'll manage,' said the Doctor cheerfully. 'Now go, we'll only slow you down.'

Sarah knew it was no time to argue. She nodded and ran off, slipping quickly through the trees. The Doctor grabbed the inert form of Warlock and hoisted it over his shoulder. In the process he dislodged his hat, which dropped softly to the leaves underfoot. Not bothering to pick it up, the Doctor set off after Sarah at a stumbling run.

Minutes later, Namin came through the trees, the Mummy just behind him. The Egyptian's eyes gleamed in triumph at the sight of the battered broad-brimmed hat on the ground. He turned to the Mummy, and made a sweeping gesture. 'Circle around the edge of the wood and get ahead of them.'

Moving swiftly despite its huge bulk, the Mummy stalked away. Namin drew his gun, and set off on the trail of the Doctor.

Stumbling and gasping for breath, Sarah ran on through the woods. Through the trees she saw a high brick wall, a pair of heavy iron gates and a low cottage-like building just inside them. Sarah gave a gasp of relief and started to run faster. Suddenly she heard a thunderous crashing sound coming towards her. She dived for the cover of a clump of bushes, wriggling deep inside them. From her hiding place she saw with amazement the giant form of an Egyptian Mummy stalking along. Somehow it had got ahead of her. Now it was moving back through the woods— towards the Doctor and Warlock. Instinctively Sarah moved to warn them—then stopped. There was nothing she could do. Better to obey the Doctor's original instructions and get help from the Lodge. She ran towards the little building.

In the heart of the wood, the Doctor stumbled on. Warlock was a big heavy man, and with such a burden even the Doctor couldn't move very fast. Nor could he watch his footing. He stepped on a dry branch, and it cracked with a noise like a pistol-shot. The Doctor paused, listening. In the woods behind him Namin, gun in hand, stood listening too. He smiled in satisfaction, and went on, following the direction of the noise.

Suddenly the Doctor heard the sounds of close pursuit. Wearily he lowered Warlock to the ground. What was he to do now? There was no real cover near by, and unless he abandoned the wounded Warlock, no hope of running.

The Doctor stood quite still, listening keenly. For a moment the noises stopped too, then they began again. The Doctor was as motionless as any Indian warrior, trying to sort out the meaning of the sounds.

There were two pursuers, he decided. The smaller one was behind him moving quickly and fairly quietly. The larger was somewhere ahead, crashing through the bushes with no attempt at concealment.

The Doctor guessed the smaller one was Namin. But the larger ... he had no idea. Clearly Namin had called on some huge and powerful ally.

The Doctor went on listening. The two pursuers were moving through the woods in a regular search pattern, trying to trap him in a kind of pincer movement. Alone he could have slipped between them with ease. But with the weight of a very heavy wounded man on his back, flight was out of the question.

The only remaining chance was concealment. There was a clump of particularly thick bushes not far away. Shouldering Warlock, who was moaning and breathing stertorously, the Doctor moved towards them. The thick branches and leaves made a kind of cave, and the Doctor crawled inside dragging Warlock after him. He settled down to wait.

Gun in hand Namin ran through the woods. He knew the fugitives wouldn't travel very fast, burdened as they were with a wounded man. Namin's plan was simple. He hoped to drive the Doctor and his friends into the arms of the Mummy. If it caught them, it would dispose of them soon enough. And if he himself got a clear sight of them, he would simply shoot them down.

In his hiding place, the Doctor lay quietly waiting. Beside him Warlock moaned, and the Doctor put a gentle hand over his lips to quiet him.

From outside, the Doctor heard the sound of approaching movement. As if guided by some uncanny instinct, *both* his pursuers seemed to be making straight for his hiding place. He was trapped.

3

The Servants of Sutekh

A deep, booming sound echoed through the woods, like crashing discords from some enormous organ. In their different parts of the wood, Namin and the Mummy stopped dead. Namin turned to face the house, his face exultant. 'The all-powerful one descends. Oh noble god, your servant hears your voice.' He started running towards the house. At the same moment, the Mummy began stalking in the same direction.

The Doctor listened, puzzled, as the sound of Namin's movements suddenly moved *away* from him. The second pursuer, the larger one, was moving too. The sound came closer, then died away, as it moved past him somewhere just out of sight.

The Doctor was about to pick up Warlock when he heard someone else coming towards him. He grabbed a fallen branch for a club and stood ready to defend himself. He tossed it aside with relief as Sarah and a small round-faced man appeared through the trees. Sarah performed breathless introductions. 'Doctor, this is Laurence Scarman. Mr Scarman, this is the Doctor.'

Laurence gave the Doctor a puzzled look, then moved straight to his old friend. 'Oh the poor chap,' he said fussily. 'Is he badly hurt? What should we do?'

'Get him somewhere safe and stop the bleeding,' suggested the Doctor practically.

Laurence nodded. 'Yes, of course. We'll take him back to the Lodge.'

The Doctor and Laurence raised Warlock between them, and began half-carrying, half-dragging him away. Sarah moved close to the Doctor. 'Listen,' she whispered, 'I saw a Mummy. A walking Mummy!'

'Nonsense, Sarah. Mummies are eviscerated, embalmed corpses. They do not walk.'

'But I tell you I *saw* one.'

'Never mind that now,' said the Doctor impatiently. 'Give Mr Scarman a hand, Sarah. I've just remembered, I lost my hat! Be with you in a moment.' The Doctor strode away.

Sarah glared furiously after him, opened her mouth, shut it again, and helped Laurence carry Warlock towards the Lodge.

Distantly from the house they heard the deep rolling notes of the organ.

Inside the sitting room of the Lodge, Laurence fussed round with towels, bandages and hot water, while the Doctor, now returned with his recovered hat, swiftly and efficiently dressed Warlock's wound.

When Warlock was comfortably settled on an enormous sofa, his shoulder bandaged and his arm in a sling, Sarah had time to look around her. It was evident that if his brother was obsessed with Egypt's past, Laurence Scarman's interests were all turned towards the future, and particularly the future of Science. The sitting room was cluttered with a variety of scientific devices, most of them obviously rigged-up by Laurence himself. The heavy old-fashioned equipment, with its brass and mahogany fittings, was the kind of thing

Sarah remembered seeing on childhood visits to the Science Museum.

Warlock's eyes flickered open, and Sarah leaned over him.

'How do you feel? Is there anything I can get you?'

Warlock looked vaguely at her. Sarah guessed he was suffering from delayed shock. 'No ... no ...' he muttered. 'I'm all right now ... must rest.' His head nodded and his eyes closed.

'That's right, have a good sleep,' said Sarah gently. She settled him comfortably on the pile of sofa cushions.

The Doctor, meanwhile, was prowling interestedly round the room, peering at the various pieces of equipment. He looked up as he saw Laurence Scarman heading for the door. 'Where are you off to, old chap?'

'To fetch the police, of course. I mean, in view of what you've been telling me ...'

The Doctor shook his head reprovingly. 'No, no, no, Mr Scarman, this is much too grave a matter for the police.'

Laurence gaped at him. 'Too grave for the police?'

The Doctor nodded solemnly. 'I'm afraid they would only hinder my investigations.'

Once again Laurence could only repeat the Doctor's words unbelievingly. '*Your* investigations?'

'That's right. Why do you think I'm here? Someone is interfering with Time, Mr Scarman—and Time is my business.'

Laurence moved away from the door, staring at the Doctor in total bafflement. 'Look here,' he demanded a little peevishly, 'who *are* you?'

37

Absorbed in a piece of equipment, the Doctor didn't seem to hear him. Sarah felt politeness demanded some sort of reply.

'I'm Sarah Jane Smith,' she said brightly, 'I'm a journalist.'

Laurence looked at her sceptically. 'A journalist—I see! And your companion?'

'Oh he's—well he's just the Doctor. We travel in time, you see—I'm from the future.'

Laurence sighed and scratched his head. 'This is all utterly preposterous, Miss Smith.'

'Yes it is, isn't it,' agreed Sarah sympathetically. 'I'm sorry.'

The Doctor had moved to yet another piece of equipment. 'This is a most interesting contraption,' he said affably. He was looking at a glass dome which covered a number of complicated-looking valves, and a paper-roll on which rested an ink-stylus.

Laurence bustled over to him. 'Kindly leave that alone,' he said severely. 'It is a delicate piece of apparatus, the purpose of which you do not understand. Furthermore, it contains a highly dangerous electrical charge!'

'So I perceive,' said the Doctor. 'What year is this?'

Laurence stared at him. 'Year?'

'Simple enough question surely?'

'Are you telling me you don't even know the year?'

'If I knew I wouldn't ask, would I? Don't be obtuse, man!'

Laurence controlled himself with an obvious effort. 'The year is nineteen-eleven,' he said stiffly.

The Doctor beamed at him. 'Oh splendid, an excellent year. I really must congratulate you, Mr Scarman. You've invented the radio telescope about forty years too early!'

'That sir,' said Laurence with dignity, 'happens to be a Marconiscope. Its purpose is——'

'—to record emissions from the stars,' completed the Doctor.

Laurence gave him a wondering look. 'Now how could you possibly know that?'

The Doctor smiled. 'Well, you see, Mr Scarman, I have the advantage of being a little ahead of you. Sometimes behind you, but normally ahead of you.'

'I see.'

'No you don't, but it's nice of you to try. Now, suppose you show me how this gadget of yours works?'

Laurence's scientific pride overcame his bewilderment. 'You'd like me to demonstrate?'

'If you please.'

Laurence bent over the glass dome and flicked a number of brass switches. Immediately the Marconiscope began to hum with power, and the valves glowed brightly. The roll of paper started to revolve, and the stylus traced out a jerky pattern. 'Amazing!' said the Doctor softly.

Laurence smiled shyly. 'You're very kind, Doctor.' He flicked more switches and then looked up in alarm. 'I can't switch it off!'

The valves glowed more fiercely, the power-hum rose in pitch, and the cylinder of paper began to revolve faster and faster. Suddenly a valve burst with a sharp crack, and the Marconiscope juddered to a halt, giving out clouds of smoke. The Doctor fanned away the fumes with his hat. Sarah coughed and said, 'Very impressive.'

Laurence shook his head. 'Extraordinary. It's never done that before.'

The Doctor lifted off the glass dome and carefully removed the paper cylinder. 'Fascinating,' he muttered. 'A regular pattern, repeated over and over again.'

Sarah was puzzled. 'Like an SOS, you mean?'

The Doctor looked thoughtfully at her. 'I wonder ... Where was your apparatus trained, Mr Scarman? Would it have been on Mars?' When Laurence nodded, the Doctor produced a small device from his pocket. He touched an inset control, and a long aerial extended itself. The Doctor adjusted more controls. 'I just want to verify the signal. No harm in double checking.' He touched a switch and the instrument began to give out a rapid regular beep, beep, beep.

Laurence looked on in fascination. 'What *is* that thing, Doctor?'

'In principle, exactly the same device that you've invented, my dear fellow. Perhaps a little less ... cumbersome.' The Doctor listened to the beeping for a few minutes, then nodded, satisfied. 'Yes, it's the same signal all right.' He switched off the device, retracted the aerial and stowed the whole thing away in his pocket. 'Now then, pencil and paper if you please.'

Laurence hurried to provide them. 'What are you going to do?'

'Decipher the message. It shouldn't take long. They'd try to make it easy.'

'Who would?'

Absorbed in his calculations, the Doctor didn't seem to hear him. 'Now let me see … *this* pattern recurs three times in one line, so we'll call that "E" …'

Sarah answered Laurence's question. 'Whoever transmitted the message, I suppose.'

The Doctor's pencil sped across the paper, filling page after page with rapid calculations. Laurence and Sarah looked on, not daring to speak. At last the Doctor threw down his pencil. His face was grim. 'Got it. It says *"Beware Sutekh!"* '

'Who's Sutekh?' asked Sarah.

The Doctor was pacing about the room, his eyes staring into some unimaginable distance. 'He may be better known to you as Set,' he said absently.

Sarah struggled to summon up her knowledge of Egyptology. Long ago she'd researched an article on Egyptian mythology for some educational magazine … 'Wasn't Set one of the Egyptian gods? He was defeated in a great battle with Horus, the god of light.'

The Doctor nodded. 'That's right. If my theories are correct, your world may be facing the greatest peril in its history.' He strode briskly towards the door.

'Hey, wait for me,' called Sarah.

The Doctor paused in the doorway. His voice was grave. 'No, Sarah. The forces that are being summoned into corporal existence in that house are more powerful and more dangerous than anything we've ever encountered. Stay here.'

'I've got a hunting rifle,' offered Laurence. 'It might come in useful.'

'Certainly not,' said the Doctor severely. 'I *never* carry firearms.' And with that he was gone.

41

Laurence turned to Sarah. 'I think we *ought* to go with him. And I should feel better if I brought a rifle.'

'So should I,' said Sarah grimly. 'Bring it!'

She waited impatiently while Laurence fished the rifle from a cluttered cupboard, which held several other guns. There was a further wait while he found the ammunition and loaded the rifle. When at last all was ready, they hurried off after the Doctor.

Night was falling as the Doctor hurried through the shadowy woods. As he neared the house, the deep throbbing notes of the organ grew louder. The hideous, discordant sounds shattered the peace of the night. Still the noise had its use, thought the Doctor. It would at least cover his approach. He went boldly up to the front door, only to find it locked. A few minutes work with his picklock took care of that. The door creaked open and the Doctor slipped into the darkened house, moving along the gloomy passages.

All was dark until he came to the organ room. An eerie green glow was shining from beneath its door. The noise of the organ was terrifying. It seemed as if the old house might be shaken to pieces by the vibration. The Doctor moved to the door, opened it a crack and peered inside.

Namin sat at the organ, hammering at the keys in an exalted trance. Three of the giant Mummies stood around the alcove in a half-circle. Their bandaged arms were raised as though invoking some mystic power. The fierce unearthly green glow came from the ornate urn-flanked Casket, in its special alcove. It filled the room with an eerie flickering light. Suddenly the lid of the Casket seemed to shimmer and dissolve. It was replaced by a spinning Vortex, a kind of whirlpool in space. The Doctor thought to himself that it was like staring down an immensely long tunnel into the eye of a typhoon. The tremendous energy from the Casket dominated the room. It seemed impossible to look anywhere else.

Namin stopped playing and knelt before the swirling Casket. Now, as if in reply, the deep throbbing discords seemed to come from the Casket itself. Namin raised his arms in prayer. 'All-high, all-powerful, most noble Master,' he chanted. 'Thy humble servant welcomes thee.'

Far away at the end of the tunnel a figure appeared. It wore black robes, a shining globe covered its head, and its feet were bare. It rushed closer and closer until it filled the entrance to the Casket ...

As the Doctor looked on in fascination, he heard a whisper beside him. 'Doctor ...' It was Sarah. Beside her was Laurence Scarman. Totally absorbed, the Doctor waved them to silence. They crouched beside him, peering through the crack. The black-robed figure stepped from the Casket. With a thrill of horror, Sarah saw that its bare feet left charred, smoking footprints on the carpet.

Namin knelt before the figure, his face to the ground. 'Master, at last you are here. I, Ibrahim Namin, and my forebears have served you faithfully through all the years that you have slept. We have guarded the secret of your tomb ...'

The figure spoke. Its voice was cold and dead. 'Stand. Look upon my face.'

43

Namin's voice trembled. 'Oh Great One, Lord Sutekh ... I dare not.'

'Look,' the cold voice commanded again. 'Is this the face of Sutekh?'

Shuddering, Namin looked up. As the figure advanced towards him, he cringed back in sudden fear. 'Oh Master, spare me,' he shrieked. 'Spare me! I am a true servant of the great Sutekh.'

The figure's hands clamped down on Namin's shaking shoulders. Immediately Namin's whole body twisted. He let out a shuddering scream and struggled to break free. His clothing began to smoulder beneath the figure's hands.

'I am the servant of Sutekh,' the dead voice said. 'He needs no other.'

Namin struggled wildly, but the fiery grip was strong as steel. 'Die!' said the voice. 'I bring Sutekh's gift of death to all humanity.'

4

The Return of Marcus Scarman

The hands released their grip, and the still-smoking body dropped to the floor. Death was Ibrahim Namin's reward for a lifetime of faithful service. The black-robed figure glowed and *changed*. Its new form was that of a tall, thin man, with a scholarly face. He wore a white suit, stiff collar and public-school tie. His face was ghastly, with greyish skin, bloodless lips and red-rimmed eyes that burned like fiery coals. It was a face that meant nothing to the Doctor and Sarah. But Laurence Scarman recognised it instantly. 'It's *Marcus*,' he whispered. 'That's my brother Marcus——' The Doctor grabbed Laurence's arm in a painful grip, and touched a warning finger to his lips. Laurence fell silent.

For a moment it seemed as if Marcus Scarman might have heard the whisper from outside the door. The burning eyes swept swiftly round the room. Then, apparently satisfied, he turned to the waiting Mummies. 'Take the generator loops. Place them in position at the compass points. Activate at ground strength.' Each of the three Mummies picked up one of the urns flanking the Casket. Scarman himself picked up the fourth.

As the strange procession headed for the door the Doctor whispered, 'Quick, everybody. Hide!'

When Marcus flung open the organ-room doors, the passage was empty. He led the Mummies along it, into the hall and out of the front door. In the passage, the Doctor slid his long body from a cramped position behind a grandfather clock, and opened the lid of a large oak chest. Laurence climbed out, followed by Sarah. She looked round. 'Where have they gone?'

'To set up a deflection shield around the house. It'll take them a while. Obviously he's planned every step.'

Laurence said unbelievingly, 'Who has? Marcus?'

The Doctor shook his head. 'No. Sutekh.' He led them into the organ room. 'Sutekh is breaking free his ancient bonds. If he succeeds, he'll destroy the world.'

'So Sutekh wasn't destroyed by Horus?' asked Sarah. 'He's still—alive?'

The Doctor went over to the Casket, and knelt to examine it more closely. 'He destroyed his own planet, Phaester Osiris, and left a trail of havoc across half the galaxy. Horus and the other Osirians must have cornered him on Earth.'

'In Egypt,' said Sarah, still struggling to understand. 'What you're saying is that Horus and Set and all the other Egyptian gods were really immensely powerful aliens from some other planet. When they came to Earth, the Egyptians worshipped them as gods.'

The Doctor nodded, running his sonic screwdriver along the side of the Casket. 'The war of the gods entered into Egyptian mythology. In fact their whole Egyptian culture was founded on the Osirian pattern.'

Laurence Scarman had been listening uncomprehendingly. 'I'm afraid all this is beyond me.'

'Don't worry,' said Sarah consolingly. 'Most of it's beyond me too.'

There was a triumphant exclamation from the Doctor. 'Ah, found it.' He removed a concealed panel on the side of the Casket, exposing a maze of complex circuitry. 'This is the lodestone that drew the TARDIS off course.'

Laurence peered fascinatedly at the circuits. 'What is it?'

'The entrance to a Space/Time tunnel,' replied the Doctor solemnly.

Sarah came over to look. 'Leading where?'

'To Sutekh,' said the Doctor, cautiously adjusting a circuit. Suddenly his fiddling produced dramatic results. The spinning Vortex reactivated, the organ-noise boomed out, and the Doctor was dragged closer and closer to the mouth of the Space/Time tunnel.

'Stay back,' he yelled. Sarah and Laurence looked on helplessly. Struggling desperately, the Doctor was sucked closer and closer to the Vortex. Clinging to the edge of the Casket with one hand, he used the other to whip the TARDIS key from its chain around his neck and swing it across the Casket's mouth. There was a bang, a brilliant flash and the Vortex died away. The force of the explosion flung the Doctor backwards across the room.

Sarah and Laurence ran across to the body. The Doctor was quite unconscious. Sarah knelt down, trying to revive him. 'Doctor, come on. Wake up, please!' The Doctor didn't stir.

Laurence shook his head. 'It's no use. He took the full force of the blast.'

Sarah looked round anxiously. 'They're bound to come back soon.'

'We could try carrying him to the lodge,' suggested Laurence.

Sarah shook her head. 'We'd be too slow. We'd probably meet those Mummy things just outside the house. We've got to find somewhere to hide him.'

Laurence's face lit up. 'Wait—there is a place. If I can still find it ...' He crossed to one wall and began running his fingers over the moulding of the oak panelling.

Sarah watched, puzzled. 'In here?'

'Somewhere here. Marcus and I discovered it as boys. We called it the priest's hole.' Suddenly a section of wall slid back, revealing a small black opening. 'There it is. There's a kind of room inside. It's not very large I'm afraid.'

Sarah looked dubiously down at the Doctor. 'And he is! Help me get him inside.' They started to drag the Doctor's inert body towards the panelling.

At dawn the following day, Ernie Clements was slipping quietly through the woods around the Old Priory. The deep pockets of his coat concealed traps, snares and a sack, and he carried a folding shot-gun. Ernie was a poacher, who took an almost professional pride in his work. He had long regarded the Old Priory estate as his own personal preserve. With Mr Laurence all wrapped up in his new-fangled experiments, and Mr Marcus away in Egypt half the time, there was no one to take care of the game on the estate.

Who would look after the partridges and pheasants, and keep the rabbits under control, if Ernie didn't see to it? He regarded himself as the Scarmans' unpaid gamekeeper. Now, whistling silently, Ernie was moving through the woods, giving his traps a final check before going back to his cottage for a well-earned rest.

Suddenly he heard the snap of a trap, and a low inhuman snarl. One of his traps had caught something —and the something sounded very much larger than a rabbit. Ernie slipped through the trees in the direction of the noise. Peering round a thick tree-trunk he froze in unbelieving horror. A giant bandage-wrapped figure was thrashing about and roaring, its huge foot caught in one of Ernie's traps.

Ernie stared at it in amazement. One of them Egyptian mummy things, wasn't it? He'd seen pictures of them on occasional visits to the house. But those things were supposed to be dead. This one was very much alive and very angry.

After struggling furiously for a few minutes, the creature wrenched the stake chain from the ground and prised open the jaws of the trap. Releasing its foot, it hurled the trap crashing against a tree. Then it turned and stalked back towards the house.

Shaken and trembling Ernie watched it go. He picked up the trap. The metal was mangled and twisted. Dropping it quickly, Ernie turned and ran for his life, vowing that he'd never poach again.

Ernie had reached the edge of the wood around the estate when he ran into his second shock of the morning. He ran into it quite literally—it was an invisible wall. There was a crackle of static power and *some-*

thing threw him back. He slowly picked himself up, recovered his gun and moved cautiously forward, hands outstretched. At the same point he felt a shock as his hands touched an invisible wall of energy. Hurriedly he drew them back. He picked up a pebble, tossed it. The pebble bounced back—off nothing. Scratching his head, Ernie turned back the way he had come. Frowning thoughtfully he made his way across through the woods, keeping well out of sight of the house. He was moving east, planning to take refuge in his old hut, just on the borders of the estate. Well, it wasn't *his* hut, exactly. He'd found it abandoned and half ruined, so he'd patched it up and taken it over.

But Ernie wasn't able to reach his hut. On the eastern edge of the estate he ran into the same invisible wall, with the same painful results. This time he made the mistake of taking a run at it. He finished up on his back several yards away, winded and shocked. Ernie picked himself up disgustedly. But he wasn't going to give up. This time he worked his way *along* the wall. He came to one of those Egyptian urn things—someone must have carried it out from the house. The urn seemed to hum, and was warm to the touch. Ernie decided to leave it alone. But he made an interesting discovery. At the urn, the invisible wall made a right hand turn—he was on the inside of an invisible corner. Doggedly Ernie traced the course of the wall. It took him a long time because the wall enclosed the entire estate. And there was an urn standing at each invisible corner ...

Realising at last that there was no escape, north,

south, east *or* west, Ernie decided there was only one thing for it. He'd go down to the Lodge and have a word with Mr Laurence. For all the fact that his head was full of this scientific mumbo-jumbo, Mr Laurence was a good sort. Ernie had often taken both brothers poaching their own game when they were boys. If Mr Laurence *had* invented an invisible wall, he'd just have to turn it off so Ernie could go home. And he certainly ought to be told about that Mummy thing. Rampaging round the place, smashing a man's traps. Having convinced himself of a legitimate grievance, Ernie set off boldly for the Lodge.

Doctor Warlock woke from an uneasy, feverish sleep. He seemed to have heard someone coming into his room. His eyes opened, and it took him a while to realise where he was. Why wasn't he at his home in the village? What was he doing on a sofa in the Lodge? He tried to sit up. His shoulder ached fiercely and one arm was strapped up. Suddenly the events of the previous day came flooding back. Warlock sat up painfully. The curtains were still drawn, the room in semi-darkness. He turned up the wick of the oil lamp that burned on a table beside his couch. Then he started back. The yellow light showed a white-clad figure standing over him.

Doctor Warlock blinked and rubbed his eyes. It was Marcus. Marcus Scarman! Poor fellow looked shockingly ill, though. Skin a terrible greyish colour, eyes sunken and red-rimmed. Maybe he'd picked up one of those filthy tropical diseases out in Egypt.

'Marcus, my dear fellow,' said Doctor Warlock heartily. 'At last you're back!'

Marcus Scarman spoke coldly. 'Why are you here?'

Doctor Warlock knew at once that something was terribly wrong. The face was Marcus's, though shockingly changed, but the voice was not. It was cold, dead, utterly inhuman. Doctor Warlock had the fleeting thought that *something* was speaking through Marcus's lips. He looked at the expressionless face. 'What's the matter?' he asked gently. 'For goodness sakes, old fellow, don't you recognise me?' Perhaps the illness had affected Marcus's brain.

The burning eyes in the grey face stared at him for a long moment. Then the bloodless lips said stiffly, 'Warlock?'

'That's right,' said Doctor Warlock, encouragingly. 'Marcus, we've all been most dreadfully worried about you ...'

The dead voice interrupted him. 'I came to find the other Scarman.'

'The other—you mean Laurence, your brother?'

'The other Scarman. The human. Where is he?'

Warlock said, 'Look here, old chap, if this is some kind of macabre joke ...'

There was a definite threat in the cold voice now. 'The other Scarman, Warlock. Where is he?'

Convinced that his old friend was deranged, Doctor Warlock decided to humour him. 'Laurence went up to the house. It may interest you to know that your Egyptian servant went berserk and took a pot-shot at me. Laurence and the Doctor went off to deal with him. There was a girl with them. Plucky young thing.'

Warlock fished out his pocket watch. 'They've been gone a devil of a time. Hope nothing's amiss.'

'Who is this Doctor?'

Warlock shook his head. 'No idea. One of Laurence's friends, I imagine. Scientist chappie. I'd just been shot when I met him, so my memory's a bit hazy.'

'Why did this Doctor interfere?'

'Interfere? He probably saved my life, Marcus. Now you see here ...'

Astonishingly Marcus said, 'He should not have interfered. *All* humans within the deflection barrier are to be destroyed.'

Warlock was totally baffled. 'Great heavens, Marcus, what's wrong with you?'

Marcus Scarman turned away dismissively. 'Destroy this human.' He spoke not to Warlock, but to a giant figure that loomed out of the shadows. Warlock backed away in terror as the Mummy lumbered forward. He screamed as two great hands reached out for him. 'Marcus, no ...'

From just outside the Lodge, Ernie Clements heard the scream. The terrifying sound made him pause and dart back from the door. He flattened himself against the wall just around the corner. He watched in amazement as the Mummy came out of the Lodge and moved away. And there was a man with it. Ducking back into hiding, Ernie caught just a glimpse of someone in a white suit. Cautiously, he slipped inside the Lodge. Sprawled on the sitting-room floor he found the body of Doctor Warlock.

Ernie knelt beside it. 'Murdering swine,' he muttered. Doctor Warlock had been a good friend. He'd bought many a rabbit or partridge with no questions asked.

Confused as he was by all that had happened, one thing was clear to Ernie. The white-suited man had obviously been controlling the Mummy. Therefore *he* was responsible for Doctor Warlock's death. Angrily, Ernie loaded his shotgun and left the Lodge, determined to track down the murderer of his friend. Someone was going to pay for Warlock's death.

5

The World Destroyed . . .

Ernie Clements had no very clear idea what he was going to do as he tracked the white-suited man and his monstrous companion back to the Priory. He was just in time to see the two strange figures enter the house by the front door. 'Just as if they ruddy well owned it,' muttered Ernie.

He was still hoping to find Mr Laurence. *He* was the one who'd know what to do about all this. They were dealing with murder now after all, and Ernie's instinct was to hand over to someone equipped to deal with such things.

But he couldn't just walk into the Priory, not with this white-suited bloke and his pet monster around it. Maybe they'd taken the place over. And where was Mr Laurence, anyway? A prisoner in the house perhaps . . .

Ernie began to work his way closer to the Priory. If he could get to the shrubbery unseen, he might be able to take a look through the ground-floor windows, find out what was going on that way.

Moving with all the skill of a born poacher, Ernie slipped quietly into the shrubbery. He looked in several windows without success. All the rooms were silent and empty. He didn't even catch sight of old Collins prowling about.

When he came to the Egyptian room, Ernie had

better luck. There were lots of those Mummy things in there, taking stuff out of crates. He caught a glance of the white-suited man too. He was just going out of the door, some of the Mummies following behind him. Ernie moved along the outside of the house paralleling their course. He looked through the window of the organ room, and there they were.

He had another quick glimpse of the white-suited man, though a Mummy was blocking his view of the man's face. Then he saw one of the Mummies drag away a body. Another body! Convinced by now that he was dealing with a dangerous murderer, Ernie raised his gun to his shoulder—awaiting his chance for a clear shot at the man in white . . .

Inside the priest hole, Sarah, Laurence and the still-unconscious Doctor were crammed into the tiny room. The remainder of the night had passed very slowly. The only light came from a solitary flickering candle, last of a batch, left behind from one of the Scarmans' boyhood adventures. Sarah woke suddenly from a nightmare-ridden doze. Laurence was asleep in a corner, mouth open and snoring quietly. His eyelids fluttered, and he began to stir.

Sarah shook Laurence awake. 'Look! I think the Doctor's coming round.'

'What?' Laurence woke with a start, rubbing his hand across his eyes.

The Doctor's eyes flicked open. 'A parallax coil!' he said suddenly. 'I never expected that. A simple trap. Blew up in my face. Clever.'

Laurence shook his head. 'Delirious, poor chap.'

Sarah shushed him. 'Mustn't underestimate Sutekh.' continued the Doctor, still to himself. 'Thinks of everything.' He sat up and looked round. 'Where are we?'

'Hiding.'

'I can see that! Where?'

Laurence answered for Sarah. 'In a priest's hole.'

'In a Victorian Gothic folly?' said the Doctor severely. 'Nonsense.'

'Well we're here, aren't we?' said Sarah crossly. 'Don't be so pedantic, Doctor. If the Victorians copied the architecture, they could copy the priest's hole too. Anyway, does it matter?' Her cramped and uncomfortable night had left her tired and cross.

The Doctor wasn't listening. He stared abstractedly at the flickering candle flame. 'If only we knew Sutekh's exact physical location.' He turned to Laurence. 'Where was your brother's expedition bound for?'

'Somewhere called Sekkara, I believe. He wrote to say he'd discovered a hidden pyramid in that region. He believed it concealed what he called a mastaba, a burial chamber.'

The Doctor frowned. 'Somewhere near Sekkara ... that's pretty vague. There might be one chance ...'

'To do what?' asked Sarah.

'Stop Sutekh. With the equipment at the Lodge I could set up a jamming signal. And as Sutekh is controlling operations by mental force ...'

'You could block his power?'

'Possibly. But only if the etheric impulse was projected along precisely the right axis. Otherwise it'd be no good . . .' Suddenly his face cleared. 'The Egyptian's ring!'

'What about it?'

'It's a slave relay. Calculating the reverse polarisation will be child's play. Why didn't I think of it before?' The Doctor scrambled to his feet, ready to set off at once.

Sarah heard sounds from the other side of the thin panel. She raised her hand. 'Sssh! Listen . . .'

Peering through a crack in the panelling, Sarah saw Marcus and three Mummies re-enter the organ room. Marcus paused and pointed at the body of Ibrahim Namin. 'Remove this carcass!' One of the Mummies grabbed the body by an arm and began dragging it out. Marcus turned to the others. 'There are other humans still within these walls. Find and kill them!' The Mummies turned and marched away.

Marcus Scarman stood alone in the centre of the room. The burning red-rimmed eyes in the grey face swept around the walls. Clearly something was troubling him. Some long-buried memory was making him walk towards the secret panel . . .

'He's coming over,' breathed Sarah. Marcus was just the other side of the panel now, fingers groping for the hidden catch in the wainscoting. Sarah cowered back . . .

Ernie Clements crouched in the shrubbery outside the organ room. He watched the man in the white suit give his orders to the Mummies. Now the man was alone, his back to the window, apparently searching for something along the wall. In a sudden surge of furious rage, Ernie raised his shotgun and smashed the window with the barrel. The man whirled round to face him, and Ernie fired . . .

From her hiding place Sarah heard the crash of broken glass, and the roar of the gun. She felt the thump as Marcus Scarman was blown back against the panelling.

'What's happened?' whispered Laurence. He struggled to get up, but the Doctor stretched out a long arm and held him down.

Outside the window, Ernie saw the blast from both barrels strike the man in the chest, hurling him against the wall. He was suddenly appalled by what he had done. Shot at such close range, the man must be dead, or at least badly wounded. Then, to his horror, the man he had just killed straightened up and started moving towards him. It was Professor Scarman! Ernie *saw* the holes in Scarman's chest—then he saw them close up and disappear. His nerve broke. Dropping his gun, he turned and ran for the woods.

Scarman stood at the window, staring after him. His lips framed a silent command. 'Seek and destroy!' Almost at once, a Mummy appeared round the corner of the house and set off after the fleeing Ernie. It stumbled over the shotgun, picked it up, snapped it in two, then resumed the pursuit. Scarman turned away from the window.

From her crack, Sarah saw him look round the room once more. She was astonished to see that despite having been shot he was apparently unharmed. The incident seemed to have driven the secret panel from his mind. Marcus glanced round the room, frowned like someone trying to remember something, then turned and left the room.

Sarah waited a minute or two, and slid open the panel. She climbed stiffly out, followed by Laurence and the Doctor.

The Doctor said, 'Seems to be all clear.' He headed for the door.

Laurence scuttled after him. 'Where are we going, Doctor?'

'To find that Egyptian.' The Doctor was already out of the room, and moving along the passage.

Sarah caught up with him. 'One of those Mummy things took the body off somewhere. We can't search the whole Priory.'

'We won't have to—look.' The Doctor pointed. The dragging heels of the dead Namin had left a clear track along the floor.

The Doctor set off, his nose to the trail like an eager bloodhound, and Sarah and Laurence followed.

The trail led them along a familiar route through the corridors of the old house and towards the Egyptian room in which the TARDIS had first arrived. As they neared a corner the Doctor paused, holding up his hand. They heard a door open, and dragging footsteps. He looked cautiously round the corner. Marcus Scarman was leaving the Egyptian room, two Mummies following behind him. The Mummies were laden with strange objects. The Doctor watched the procession turn in the other direction and disappear down the corridor. When they were out of sight, he beckoned his companions on.

In the Egyptian room the piles of crates were scattered, and many had been unpacked. The body of Ibrahim Namin lay sprawled in an empty crate. The Doctor crossed over to it and removed the ornate ruby-red ring from the finger.

Sarah looked round the room, 'What do you think they're doing?'

The Doctor was examining the ring. 'I'm not really sure yet.'

Laurence peered into an open, half-empty crate. 'This is interesting, Doctor. It appears to be some kind of machinery.'

The Doctor and Sarah went over to the crate. Inside was a pile of strangely shaped metal objects. Sarah had never seen anything similar before, but the Doctor seemed to recognise them at once. 'Part of an Osirian anti-gravity drive. They must be building a rocket!'

'Egyptian Mummies building a rocket?' said Sarah sceptically. 'That's *really* crazy, Doctor.'

The Doctor smiled. 'Not really. Those aren't Mummies at all. They're service robots.'

'Robots? Then why do they look like Mummies?'

'The Osirians made them that way to keep the Egyptians in order, back in the days when they ruled as gods.'

'All right then,' persisted Sarah. 'Why are these robots building a rocket?'

'So that Sutekh can break free of the power of Horus.'

'Where's Sutekh now?'

'Exactly where Horus left him, seven thousand years ago. Trapped beneath a pyramid, powerless to move ... Listen!'

The dragging footsteps were coming back along the corridor. Instinctively the Doctor and Sarah ran for the shelter of the TARDIS, leaving Laurence looking after them in amazement. As the footsteps came nearer, the Doctor reached out a long arm and pulled him inside, closing the TARDIS door behind them both.

When Scarman and the Mummies re-entered the room it was empty, the TARDIS in its corner. Since the TARDIS had been there when he arrived, Marcus, or rather the being that now controlled him, had no curiosity about it, accepting it as part of the furniture.

Inside the TARDIS, Laurence Scarman was showing a great deal of curiosity. He stared round the brightly-lit control room with an air of bemused astonishment.

The Doctor smiled down at him. 'You're going to say it transcends the normal laws of physics?' he suggested kindly.

'I am, yes. I mean—it does,' spluttered Laurence. 'It's preposterous!'

'Yes it is, isn't it,' agreed the Doctor cheerfully. 'I often think dimensional transcendentalism is quite preposterous, but it works. Would you care to take a look around?'

'May I? May I really?'

'Please do ... but I wouldn't touch anything.'

Laurence scampered round the TARDIS like a child on its first visit to the Science Museum, uncertain where to begin. Sarah moved closer to the Doctor. 'Now we're here ... why don't you just—leave, take me back to my own time?'

'I can't.'

'Why can't you?'

'Unless Sutekh is stopped, Sarah, he'll destroy your world.'

Sarah stared at him. 'But he *didn't*, did he? I mean, we knew the world didn't end in nineteen eleven.'

The Doctor looked strangely at her. 'Do we?'

'Of course we do!'

The Doctor sighed. 'All right, Sarah. Let's see what the world looks like in your time.' His hands flickered over the controls, there was a hum of power, and the central column began rising and falling.

'I say,' said Laurence excitedly. 'This is just like one of those scientific romances by that Wells chappie!'

Their journey was a brief one. Soon the Doctor adjusted controls again, and the TARDIS came to a stop. 'Here we are, Sarah, if you want to get off.' His voice was grave.

Sarah looked doubtfully at him. But she wasn't going to back down now—not until she'd seen what was out there. She moved over to the doors, and the Doctor touched a control on his console. The doors slid open, and Sarah looked out on to a landscape of hell.

6

The Mummies Attack

Sarah saw a huge bleak, barren plain, stretching end-
lessly away, devastated by a perpetually howling dust-
storm. Here and there were a few shattered ruins. That
was all. No plants, no trees, no animals, no people, no
life of any kind. A dead world.

Shuddering, Sarah stepped back, and the Doctor
closed the doors. Angrily she said, 'That wasn't Earth.
It's all some horrible trick.'

The Doctor shook his head sadly. 'No, Sarah. That's
your world as Sutekh would leave it. A desolate planet
circling a dead sun.'

'But I don't understand. Earth *isn't* like that.'

'Every point in time has its alternative, Sarah.
You've just seen into alternative time.'

Laurence had been listening in fascination. 'Extraordinary. Are you saying that the future can be *chosen*,
Doctor?'

'Not chosen but ... *shaped*. The actions of the
present fashion the future.'

'So a man can change the course of history?'

'To a small extent. After all, the actions of many
men *are* history. But it takes a being of Sutekh's limit-
less powers to *destroy* the future.' He turned to Sarah.
'Well?'

Sarah's face was bleak. She hated the thought of returning to face the horrors they had just left. But she

was willing to do anything to prevent the Earth she knew turning into the desolate horror outside the TARDIS doors. 'We've got to go back, haven't we?'

'Yes,' said the Doctor quietly. 'We've got to go back.' His fingers moved once more over the controls.

Sarah and Laurence waited while the Doctor returned the TARDIS to nineteen eleven. He switched on the scanner—the Egyptian room was empty again. He opened the doors, and they left the TARDIS.

The Doctor led them straight towards the window and flung it open. 'Out we go—and keep down. We're heading back to the Lodge.' Sarah and Laurence climbed out and the Doctor followed, closing the window behind him. Crouching low, they ran for the cover of the woods.

Marcus Scarman was too occupied to be concerned about them. He was standing before Sutekh's Casket in the alcove. From inside the Casket came an eerie green glow. Marcus was talking to his Master. 'Several humans within the deflection barrier have been killed, but others remain.'

Sutekh's voice was soft and ferocious at the same time, like that of some great beast. 'Eliminate them!'

'The Servicers are searching for them, but this delays the assembly of the rocket.'

The voice became angry. 'Destruction of the humans must not be allowed to delay the construction of my rocket. That is of paramount importance.'

'Your orders will be obeyed, Sutekh. I shall recall two of the Servicers to the rocket assembly.'

The green glow died away. Knowing he was dismissed, Marcus Scarman turned and left the room.

Rather to their surprise, the Doctor and his friends reached the Lodge quite safely. Inside, Sarah drew back the dining-room curtains, revealing the stiffened corpse of Doctor Warlock. They lifted him on to the sofa, and Laurence spread a sheet over the body. He shook his head in horror and disbelief. 'I can't believe my brother was responsible for this. He and Warlock were the closest of friends.'

The Doctor was already at work on the Marconiscope. 'If you can manage to stop thinking of him as your brother, it will be a great deal easier for you,' he said gently. 'By the way, do you have any spare valves?'

Laurence brought some over to him. 'But Marcus *is* my brother!' he said miserably.

'Not any longer. The moment he entered Sutekh's tomb, he became totally subject to Sutekh's will. As a human being, Marcus Scarman no longer exists. He is simply a walking embodiment of Sutekh's powers. He has given the paralysed Sutekh arms and legs, a body to use as a means of escape.'

As he talked the Doctor was replacing the burnt-out valve in Laurence's Marconiscope. He began attaching leads from the tuner to the slave relay ring he had taken from Namin's body.

Sarah looked on as he worked absorbedly. 'If Sutekh is so totally evil, why didn't Horus and the other Osirians destroy him when they had the chance?'

'Against their code,' said the Doctor. 'To kill Sutekh

would have made them no better than he was. So they simply imprisoned him.'

'How?'

'Some kind of forcefield, I imagine. Controlled by a power source on Mars.'

'On *Mars*?' repeated Laurence incredulously.

The Doctor looked up. 'Of course. Remember that message we picked up? When your brother blundered into Sutekh's tomb, he triggered off the monitoring system on Mars. It sent out an automatic alarm signal.'

Sarah was beginning to work it out. 'So that rocket the Servicer Robots are building ...'

'Will be aimed at the forcefield control point on Mars. Exactly, Sarah. If that warhead hits its target, Sutekh will have succeeded in releasing himself.'

'To destroy the world,' said Laurence in a horrified tone.

'Not only this world. Anywhere that life is found ... Do you happen to have a magneto, old chap?'

Laurence stared blankly at him. 'A magneto? Yes, of course.' He went to a cupboard and started rummaging inside.

Ernie Clements was tearing through the woods at a stumbling run too frightened and too exhausted now to worry about moving quietly. He'd thought at first it would be easy to slip away from his pursuers. But the Mummies were too many and too determined.

They were quartering the woods with a methodical machine-like persistence. Since they were not flesh and blood, they didn't tire—unlike Ernie who by now was panting and exhausted. He felt like the fox at the end of a very long chase. For the first time in his life he felt some sympathy for the animals he hunted and trapped.

He leaned against a tree, his chest heaving. For one blissful moment he thought he had shaken off his pursuers. Then he heard the steady crashing through trees and bushes. They had him surrounded now, and were driving him forwards as a beater drives game on to the guns.

Just one thing gave Ernie a vestige of hope. They seemed to be chasing him in the direction of the Lodge, and that was the very place he wanted to be. He still had hopes that Mr Laurence would turn up to help and advise him. And even if he didn't the Lodge was a sturdy old building. Maybe he could barricade himself inside. Ernie remembered something else. There were guns in the Lodge too. They'd belonged to the Scarman boys' father, a big-game hunter in his day. Give him a nice heavy hunting rifle, Ernie thought grimly, and he'd soon show those Egyptian horrors a thing or two. They'd *need* bandages by the time he was done with them.

Fortified by this resolve, and with at least some of his breath back, Ernie set off on a last desperate dash for safety. Only one thing worried him. The trees didn't go right up to the Lodge. For the final dash he'd be in open country and in plain sight.

Ernie's luck held good till almost the last minute. He reached the edge of the woods and set off on his final run. But just as he left cover, two Mummies emerged from the woods, one to each side of him. Snarling angrily, they set off after him. They were very close, but Ernie reckoned he could just about make it ...

Sarah looked on as the Doctor finished connecting the Marconiscope to the ring. 'What are you going to do with that thing?'

'Block the mental beam that transmits Sutekh's power. He'll be helpless then.'

Sarah was struck by a thought. 'What will happen to Marcus Scarman?'

'He'll simply collapse.'

'You mean—die?'

The Doctor nodded, testing the connection on one of the leads. 'He's not alive now, in any real sense. Only the will of Sutekh animates him. And deprived of his outside contact, Sutekh will be as powerless as the day Horus imprisoned him.' The Doctor looked round. 'The main power switch is over beside the door, Sarah—I'll stay by the Marconiscope to calibrate, you throw the switch when I give the word.'

Over by the cupboard, Laurence Scarman stood listening to the low voices. He found the magneto at last and took it over to the Doctor, who looked up. 'Did you find one, old chap?'

Laurence nodded slowly. 'Here you are, Doctor.' Almost reluctantly, he handed it over.

The Doctor began wiring it in. 'Splendid.' He looked up at Laurence. 'Is there anything——'

A terrified scream came from just outside the Lodge, and grabbing his rifle, Laurence tore out of the room, through the hall and to the front door. He saw Ernie

Clements running from the woods, two pursuing Mummies converging on him. Even as Laurence watched, the little poacher stumbled and fell. Ernie picked himself up and went on running, but the delay was fatal. The two giant Mummies slammed together Ernie Clements jammed between them. His final scream of terror was cut off abruptly, and he dropped to the ground, all life crushed from his body.

Laurence Scarman threw his hunting rifle to his shoulder, and fired. One of the Mummies staggered and turned back towards the Lodge, growling with rage. The other followed. As the two horrible shapes stalked closer, Laurence fired again and again. The Mummies staggered a little as the bullets struck, but still lurched remorselessly forwards. They were almost upon Laurence when the Doctor appeared in the doorway.

'Come on, man, inside,' he yelled. He grabbed hold of Laurence and heaved him back into the house, slamming and barring the door. Ignoring Laurence's protests, he bustled him into the sitting room, shutting and locking that door too. Releasing the little man abruptly, the Doctor made a final check of the rejigged Marconiscope. There came a shattering crash as the front door gave way to the Mummies' onslaught. The Doctor made a final delicate adjustment. 'Switch on the power, Sarah.' he yelled. Already the Mummies were battering at the sitting-room door.

Just as Sarah was about to switch on, Laurence Scarman threw himself upon her, pulling her away. 'No, don't,' he cried. 'I heard what you said. You'll kill my brother!'

The door began to splinter and the Doctor rammed a heavy armchair against it. 'Sarah, switch on!' he shouted.

Sarah struggled desperately to break away from the frenzied Laurence, while the Doctor fought to keep the Mummies out of the room. Once the switch was thrown and Sutekh's mental beam blocked, the Mummies, like Marcus Scarman, would simply collapse ...

Just as Sarah tore free from Laurence, there was a splintering crash and the first of the Mummies forced its way into the room. The Doctor closed with it immediately, and actually managed to hold it for a moment. Then the Mummy threw him across the room, and lurched forward. It stumbled over the chair and into the Marconiscope—just as Sarah pulled the switch.

There was a crackle of electricity, a bang and a flash. Blue sparks arced across the Mummy's body and it dropped to the floor. But by now the second Mummy was in the room. Laurence Scarman made a brave but futile attempt to hold it. It smashed him to one side and bore down on Sarah ...

7

The Doctor Fights Back

Sarah cowered away as the Mummy loomed threateningly over her. On the far side of the room, the Doctor was struggling to his feet. Sarah heard his voice, 'The ring, Sarah! Find the ring!'

She looked round frantically. There was a red gleam among the ruins of the shattered Marconiscope. Snatching the ring she held it up before the advancing Mummy and shouted, 'Stop!' To her astonished relief, the Mummy stopped.

'Tell it to return to Control,' called the Doctor.

'Return to Control,' ordered Sarah nervously. The Mummy turned and lumbered from the room. Sarah collapsed into a chair.

The Doctor was on his feet, helping the half-stunned Laurence to get up. 'Are you all right?'

Laurence rubbed his head. 'I think so ...'

'Then you don't deserve to be,' said the Doctor angrily. 'You nearly got us all killed! What's worse, you've wrecked my only chance of stopping Sutekh.'

'Forgive me, Doctor. I just couldn't face the thought of killing my own brother.'

The Doctor crossed over to Laurence and put a hand on his shoulder. 'Now listen to me,' he said firmly. 'That thing walking about out there is no longer your brother. It is simply a human cadaver, animated by the power of Sutekh. Do you understand that?'

Laurence nodded, unable to speak. Sarah couldn't help feeling sorry for him. Whatever the Doctor said, it couldn't be easy for Laurence to accept that what looked like his brother was really the puppet of some alien power.

The Doctor moved towards the door. 'If Sutekh succeeds in freeing himself,' he warned, 'the consequences will be incalculable. Somehow we've *got* to stop him ...'

As the Doctor strode from the room, Laurence looked at Sarah. 'Where's he going?'

'To see what Sutekh's up to, I suppose. I'd better go with him.' Sarah hurried after the Doctor. Laurence collapsed into a chair, his face in his hands.

Sutekh, at that particular moment, was once again in conference with his servant Marcus Scarman. 'I detected electro-magnetic radiation,' Sutekh snarled. 'There was a deliberate attempt to block my cytronic control.'

Marcus Scarman bowed his head before the green glow from the Casket. 'I know nothing of this, Sutekh.'

'The source of power was *within* the deflection barrier.'

Marcus frowned in thought. 'There are still some humans alive within the barrier. Warlock spoke of one called the Doctor—and a girl. There is still the other Scarman, Laurence. I can order the Servicers to hunt them down and destroy them, but that will delay work on the missile.'

Sutekh's response was immediate. 'No! The missile must be fired at the appointed time. Immediately after, you will find and kill these humans.'

Marcus bowed his head. 'As you order, Sutekh, so shall it be.' The green glow faded.

Sarah and the Doctor worked their way cautiously through the woods, back towards the Priory. As they came nearer, the Doctor spotted huge figures moving to and fro in the yard behind the house. 'There they are,' he whispered. 'Let's take a closer look.' Wriggling forwards on their stomachs, they worked their way as near to the yard as they dared, stopping behind the cover of a dense clump of bushes. Sarah raised her head and peered through the leaves. She saw an opaque Pyramid made from some material that looked like heavy plastic. One side had an entrance hatch, with a ramp leading to the ground. As they watched, a Mummy came out of the hatch, walked down the ramp and moved back towards the house. Another Mummy appeared from the house, cradling in its arms a heavy metal object. It climbed the ramp and disappeared inside the Pyramid.

Sarah whispered in the Doctor's ear. 'That Pyramid thing—what is it?'

'An Osirian war missile. Almost completed by the look of it.'

'You mean that thing *flies*?'

'It transposes the power of Sutekh's will. You might call it Pyramid power.'

Marcus came round the corner of the house and stopped just by the Pyramid. Sarah had a nasty feeling he was staring straight at their hiding place. After a moment he climbed the Pyramid ramp and disappeared inside. Sarah and the Doctor slipped away, retracing their tracks to the Lodge.

They found Laurence staring sadly at an old family photograph, two solemn-faced little boys in wing collars and knickerbocker suits. He put the photograph down and looked up eagerly. 'Did you learn anything?'

'Only that time is short,' said the Doctor. He crossed to the electrocuted Mummy, sprawled face-down on the floor, and studied the pyramid shape on its back. 'Cytronic induction,' he said thoughtfully.

Sarah said, 'Come on, Doctor. Explain.'

'The Servicer robots are drawing their energy from a cytronic particle accelerator—which must be in Sutekh's tomb. After all, he's had seven thousand years to build one.'

'So?'

'So—put that out of action and he'd have no workforce, and no missile.'

Laurence broke in, 'But Sutekh's tomb is somewhere in Egypt. How could you possibly . . .'

The Doctor was striding about the room. 'Marcus came from Egypt, didn't he? Through the Space/Time tunnel. And it must be a two-way mechanism.'

Her worst fears confirmed, Sarah said, 'If you go through that tunnel, Doctor, Sutekh will kill you.'

The Doctor didn't reply—mainly because he knew there was a very good chance that Sarah was right. But if there was no alternative ...

Timidly Laurence said, 'Wouldn't it be better——'

'No it wouldn't,' snapped the Doctor, and made for the door. Then he paused. He didn't really want to go through that Time tunnel. Not if there really was some other way ... He came back into the room and sat down. 'Well,' he said grumpily. 'Wouldn't *what* be better?'

Laurence took a deep breath. 'Wouldn't it be less risky just to blow up the missile?'

'Of course it would,' said the Doctor crossly. 'But what with?'

Sarah could see that Laurence was anxious to redeem himself. 'What about blasting gelignite?' he suggested eagerly.

The Doctor looked at him in surprise. 'I suppose you just happen to have some about the place?'

'Well, no. But I do know poor Ernie Clements kept a supply in his hut. I'm afraid he used it for fishing?'

Sarah looked puzzled. 'How do you fish with gelignite?'

'You set it off and chuck it in the water,' said the Doctor. 'The underwater explosion kills the fish and they float up to the surface. It's a deplorable method, but very effective.'

Laurence nodded. 'That's right,' he confirmed, 'I heard poor Ernie "fishing" just a few night's ago.'

The Doctor rubbed his chin. 'And where did he keep this gelignite?'

'I'm not absolutely sure. But he had an old hut on the east side of the woods. That would be the obvious place.'

The Doctor made up his mind and stood up. 'Come on, Sarah.'

'I'll come with you, shall I?' offered Laurence. 'I could show you the way.'

The Doctor said quickly, 'It's all right, we'll find it.'

Laurence stopped. 'You think I'll let you down again, don't you?'

Since this was precisely what the Doctor *did* think, he was somewhat at a loss for an answer. After a moment he said gently, 'Mr Scarman, if you really want to help, you might start getting the binding off that Servicer robot.'

The Doctor left. Sarah gave Laurence a quick smile of sympathy, and followed him out.

Laurence watched them go, a worried frown on his face. He fished an old clasp-knife from a drawer, and knelt by the collapsed robot. Cautiously, he started to saw away at its bandaging.

Sarah and the Doctor were moving eastwards through the woods when suddenly the Doctor stopped. He picked up a long branch and started waving it about in front of him. Sarah stared. 'What are you doing, Doctor?'

'Being careful. Walking into a deflection barrier is like walking into an invisible wall. Painful.'

'I'd forgotten about the barrier. You mean it's between us and the hut?' The Doctor nodded, still waving his stick about. 'Can we get through it?'

The Doctor stopped as the end of his branch brushed against the invisible forcefield. 'Ah, here we are! Now all we have to do is find the door.' Using his branch as a guide, the Doctor moved along parallel with the deflection barrier, accompanied by a mystified Sarah. He followed the invisible wall until he came to an ornately decorated urn, standing incongruously beneath a tree. 'There you are,' said the Doctor happily. 'Door.' He produced his sonic screwdriver and held it up. 'Key!'

Sarah looked at him sceptically. 'As simple as that, is it?'

Regretfully the Doctor said, 'Well, no, not quite.'

Sarah groaned. 'I didn't think it could be!'

The Doctor started prodding the area round the urn with his branch. 'No obvious booby-traps, anyway.' He knelt to examine the urn more closely. After a moment, he turned and looked up at Sarah. 'Well, are you going to help, or just stand there admiring the scenery?'

'Actually I wasn't looking at the scenery,' said Sarah with dignity. She pointed down at the Doctor's boot-soles, one of which was developing a hole. 'Your shoes need repairing! Well, what do you want me to do?'

'Come and hold the base of this urn for me. And be careful—if it falls over we're done for.'

Sarah knelt on the other side of the urn, steadying it with her hands. At this close range she could hear a kind of low electronic hum. The urn vibrated slightly beneath her hands. 'Is it dangerous?' she asked nervously.

'Of course it's dangerous,' said the Doctor impatiently. He began making short, delicate sweeps across the face of the urn with his sonic screwdriver.

Nothing happened. He adjusted the screwdriver and tried again. The note from the urn started to rise. It shot up to a high-pitched electronic scream ...

The Doctor made another hasty adjustment, and the sound returned to its former level. The Doctor sat back on his heels, mopping his face with his scarf. 'Deactivating a generator loop without the correct key is like repairing a watch with a hammer and chisel. One false move and you'll never know the time again.'

'Any more comforting thoughts?' asked Sarah shakily.

'Just keep that urn steady. Oh, let me know if it starts to feel warm.'

'Don't worry, you'll know. You'll hear me breaking the sound barrier.'

The Doctor grinned and went on with his delicate task.

Far away in Egypt, in a dark cell beneath the Pyramid of Sutekh, a monitor screen occupied one wall. On the screen, four lines of light formed the pattern of a pyramid. One of these lines began flashing on and off, and a low alarm signal filled the air. From his throne, the robed, masked figure of Sutekh was looking into the monitor. 'Interference,' he snarled. 'There is interference!'

In the woods, the Doctor made a final adjustment. The sound from the urn stopped completely. Gently the Doctor unscrewed the lid of the urn, and drew out a metal cylinder. Dropping it to the ground, he stamped on it hard. 'Just to make sure,' he said cheerfully. 'Come along, Sarah.'

A thought-impulse from Sutekh triggered off the organ-like signal. Marcus came running to stand before the Casket in the Egyptian room. In Sutekh's cell, his face appeared as a flickering distorted image on the monitor. Marcus listened as Sutekh told him of the interference. 'Sutekh, I do not understand how this can be,' he protested.

'I tell you the barrier to the east has been deactivated.'

'That just isn't possible.'

'It has been deactivated,' Sutekh repeated angrily. 'The power line has gone from my monitor.'

'But the humans do not have the knowledge to shut down a deflection barrier.'

'Then it is clear that an extra-terrestial intelligence is operating against us.'

Marcus found it difficult to accept the thought. 'An extra-terrestial—an alien? Here?'

A note of insane rage came into Sutekh's voice. 'I have endured an eternity of impotent darkness. I will not be denied now. Hear my commands. You will look for the humans. But the missile is to be constantly guarded. The Servicers must maintain total vigilance.'

'All shall be as you say, Sutekh. The Servicers shall guard the missile while I check the barrier and search for your enemies.'

Sutekh's voice rose to a maddened howl. 'Once the

missile is projected, I shall seek out and destroy *all* my enemies. This alien who dares to intrude ... All the humans ... birds, fish, reptiles, plants ... *all* life is my enemy. All life shall perish under the reign of Sutekh the Destroyer!'

Marcus Scarman echoed the hideous chant. 'All life shall perish. Only Sutekh shall live!'

8

'I am Sutekh!'

Once through the deflection barrier, the Doctor and Sarah soon found Ernie Clements' hideaway. The ruined hut had never been his home. He had a comfortable cottage in the village. But the hut made a useful hiding place for guns, traps, ferrets, dead birds and rabbits, and all the other things Ernie had preferred not to keep in the cottage. Including the gelignite, used in his drastic but efficient method of fishing ...

The Doctor and Sarah came into the hut and looked around. It held an assortment of odds and ends. Crates, boxes, cages, rolls of wire, bits of traps, ricketty chairs and sagging cupboards ... It was hard to know where to start looking. They began a methodical search.

As they worked, Sarah asked, 'How powerful is Sutekh, Doctor?'

The Doctor was rummaging in an old battered chest. 'All-powerful,' he said shortly. 'If he gets free, there isn't a life-form in the galaxy able to stand against him.'

'Not even your lot—the Time Lords?'

'Not even my lot. Sutekh was only defeated in the end by the combined efforts of over seven hundred of his fellow Osirians, led by Horus.'

Sarah racked her brains to remember the article on Egyptian mythology she'd researched so long ago. 'The seven hundred and forty gods whose names are recorded in the tomb of Thutmose III, I suppose?' she said airily.

The Doctor chuckled at this display of one-upmanship. 'That's right,' he agreed. 'I'd be careful of that cage, Sarah. I think there's a ferret in it!'

Sarah opened the cage. A slim grey shape leaped out and flashed across the floor of the hut, disappearing under the door.

Sarah turned her attention to a cupboard that leaned crazily out from the wall. She groped on the top shelf and encountered what felt like soggy cardboard. She took the box down. It held cakes of some clammy substance. 'Could this be it, Doctor?' she asked, handing him the box.

The Doctor took the box without really looking. Then he straightened up, glanced inside the box and froze like a statue.

'What's the matter?' asked Sarah. 'Isn't there enough of it? It seems to have gone all soggy!' She poked the clammy stuff with one finger.

The Doctor's voice was almost unnaturally calm. 'Sarah—take your hand out of that box, very, very carefully.'

'All right,' said Sarah obligingly. 'What's the matter?'

The Doctor drew a deep breath. 'That stuff is gelignite. It's soggy because it's old and in poor condition. They call it "sweating". Sweaty gelignite is highly unstable. One good sneeze would be enough to set it off.'

Sarah stepped back hastily. 'Sorry!' she said rather inadequately.

The Doctor set the box down on the table. 'Any sign of detonators or fuses?'

Sarah rooted through the cupboard and shook her head. 'No, nothing else.' She looked back at the Doctor. 'Maybe he just used to sneeze on it?'

The Doctor scowled fiercely at her, but made no reply. Picking up the cardboard box with loving care, he led the way out of the hut.

Marcus Scarman's check of the deflector shield eventually led him to the dismantled urn. He stood looking at it for a long time. His burning gaze swept the woods around him. Then he turned and hurried away, towards the Lodge. A little later, the Doctor and Sarah appeared, following the same route to the same destination. But they were slowed by the need to move cautiously with the gelignite. They didn't see Marcus. By now he was well ahead of them.

Obeying the Doctor's rather mysterious instructions, Laurence Scarman was removing the last of the wrappings from the disabled Mummy. As they came away they revealed a kind of metallic skeleton with cross-braced metallic strips replacing pelvis and rib structure. The circular frame for the head appeared to be empty, apart from a lateral bar which was connected to the central mechanism—a pyramid of some red vitreous material.

Laurence took off the last of the wrapping and looked at the thing distastefully. Absorbed in his task, he didn't notice someone come silently into the room and stand over him.

Suddenly, warned by some instinct, he looked up. Marcus!' he said joyfully.

Marcus Scarman looked impassively down at him. Laurence rose to his feet. 'Marcus, old chap, don't you know me? I'm your brother!'

'Brother ...' Marcus spoke the word as if it had no meaning.

'That's it, I'm your brother Laurence.'

Marcus seemed to consider this for a moment. Then he said, 'As Horus was brother to Sutekh!'

Laurence's voice was low and appealing. 'Marcus, you're ill. You must let me help you.' He stretched out a hand. Marcus knocked it away with a bestial snarl.

'Trust me,' urged Laurence. 'I won't harm you.'

'Trust?' Obviously this word too was meaningless.

Laurence looked desperately round the room, seeking some way to reach his brother. He snatched up the photograph and held it out. 'Don't you remember *anything*, Marcus? Look, that's us when we were boys.'

Marcus stared down at the two young faces. Something seemed to get through to him. When he spoke again his voice held a more human note. 'Marcus ... Laurence ...' he said slowly.

'That's right. You do remember.'

'I was—Marcus.'

'And you still are,' said Laurence reassuringly. 'Now, let me help you.'

Marcus's face twisted as if in pain. 'I *was* Marcus. Now I am Sutekh!'

'No, Marcus, no. You went to Egypt, remember?

You must have fallen under some kind of mesmeric influence ...'

Marcus's voice rose to a hoarse chant. 'Sutekh the great destroyer. Sutekh the lord of death. I am his instrument ...'

Laurence spoke in a voice of desperate urgency. 'Now you listen to me, Marcus, that's all nonsense. You are *Marcus Scarman,* Professor of Archaeology, Fellow of All Souls——'

Marcus's arm swept out, knocking the picture from Laurence's hand. 'You!' he snarled contemptuously. 'What do you know of Sutekh! Where are the others?'

Laurence backed away, frightened by the sudden violence. 'What others?'

'You are being helped. The mind of Sutekh has detected an alien intelligence at work.'

'I suppose you must mean the Doctor ...'

'Doctor,' repeated Marcus in a tone of savage satisfaction. His hands shot out and seized Laurence by the shoulders. With horror Laurence saw that his brother's hands were black and charred. Their touch seemed to burn, he smelt smoke rising from his jacket. 'Marcus,' he choked, 'your hands ...'

Marcus shook him savagely. 'This Doctor ... where is he? *What is he?*' He shifted his grip to Laurence's throat.

The Doctor and Sarah crouched near the pyramid-shaped Osirian missile. Two Mummies stood guarding it like sentries. Carefully the Doctor hid the box of gelignite under a bush. 'We'll leave it there for the moment. Should be safe enough.'

Sarah gave him a sceptical look. 'You know this just isn't going to work, Doctor? No detonators, no fuses ... so even if you get near enough to place the charge without being spotted, how are we going to explode it?'

'Do stop asking silly questions,' snapped the Doctor. 'I've already thought of all that—and that's where you come in.'

Before Sarah could ask more questions, he set off for the Lodge.

When they came into the living room, Laurence Scarman was slumped in a chair, head drooping on his chest. Thinking how dejected he looked, the Doctor tried to cheer him up. He waved towards the un-wrapped Mummy framework. 'Well done, Mr Scarman. An excellent job.'

Laurence didn't respond. Sarah tapped him on the shoulder. 'Mr Scarman?'

Laurence keeled over and slumped to the floor. Sarah jumped back with a cry of shock. The Doctor knelt beside the body, then rose, shaking his head. 'Strangled, poor chap.'

'The Mummies must have come back.'

'Not this time, Sarah. There are—marks on the neck. His late brother must have called.'

'That's horrible,' said Sarah. 'He was so concerned about his brother ...'

Already the Doctor had moved away from Laurence, and was examining the exposed Mummy frame. 'Told him not to,' he said absently. 'Told him it was already too late.'

Sarah looked indignantly at him. 'Sometimes I don't

understand you, Doctor. Sometimes you don't seem——'

Sarah checked herself, and the Doctor completed her sentence for her. 'Human? You're forgetting, Sarah— I'm not.' He returned to his study of the robot mechanism. 'Splendid workmanship, this. Typical Osirian simplicity.'

Sarah could have shaken him. 'A man's just been murdered and——'

'*Five* men,' interrupted the Doctor. 'Six if you count Marcus Scarman himself. But there's no time for mourning, Sarah. Those deaths will be the first of untold millions, unless Sutekh is stopped.' He looked down at the body. 'Know thine enemy. Admirable advice. I did try to warn him, you know.'

Sarah heard the pain in his voice and realised that the Doctor was hiding his feelings under a mask of flippancy. 'All right, Doctor,' she said gently. 'What do we do now?'

'If we're going to do anything about that missile, we'll have to move quickly. I'll need your help, Sarah.'

'What do you want me to do?'

The Doctor was sorting through a pile of Mummy bindings. 'Clever chaps, the Osirians,' he said conversationally. 'These wrappings are chemically impregnated to protect the robots against damage and corrosion.' He began to wrap a binding around one leg. 'An impenetrable disguise, wouldn't you say?'

Sarah looked at him in alarm.

The Doctor smiled. 'Now then, what sort of a shot are you?'

*

While Sarah helped the Doctor to swathe himself in Mummy bindings, Marcus Scarman was supervising the other Servicer robots in their work. Two of them were lifting a heavy cylinder from one of the crates. Marcus called, 'Stop!' The Mummies stopped. Marcus examined the hieroglyphics on the side of the cylinder. This is the Warhead trigger charge, Phase One. It must be placed directly under the detonation head. Signify your understanding.' Both Mummies lowered their heads. Satisfied Scarman said, 'Continue.' The Mummies moved out of the room.

Sarah fixed the last of the wrappings around the Doctor's feet. A muffled voice said, 'Hurry up.'

'I am hurrying,' she replied indignantly. 'Don't want to come unwrapped, do you?' she fixed the wrapping in place. 'There.'

Swathed in bindings from head to foot, the Doctor made an impressively Mummy-like figure. 'That'll do,' he said. 'It doesn't have to be perfect, you know. I may have to mingle with the Mummies, but I definitely shan't linger. How do I look?'

Sarah shook her head sadly. 'It must have been a terrible accident.'

'Don't provoke me,' said the muffled voice. Lurching a little, the disguised Doctor picked up his coat, scarf and hat and moved towards the door. 'Come along, Sarah. And don't forget that rifle.'

Marcus Scarman stood before the glowing Casket, his

hands raised in supplication. 'The work on the missile is almost complete, Sutekh. We need only the target co-ordinates.'

The voice of Sutekh said, 'I shall now release them.'

The glowing Casket blurred and faded, to be replaced by the spinning Vortex of the Space/Time tunnel. Tumbling end over end, a white cylinder appeared, speeding closer and closer to Marcus until it shot from the tunnel like a projectile and rolled across the floor to his feet. Marcus bent and picked it up.

The cylinder glowed with the fire of Sutekh and there was a horrible sizzling sound as Marcus touched it. But he felt no pain. Only the living feel pain.

Sutekh ordered, 'Engage the co-ordinates in the projection dome monitor.'

'Immediately, Sutekh.' The still-smoking cylinder in his hands, Marcus turned and left the room.

Moving awkwardly because of his bindings, the Doctor took the box of gelignite from its hiding-place. Beside him, Sarah was settling into position, prone on the ground with the rifle, like someone at a firing-range. The Doctor looked down at her. 'You know what to do?'

'Give you time to get clear and—pow!'

'And be sure to shoot straight. You won't get a second shot.'

'Don't worry, Doctor. I know what I'm doing. Good luck!'

The Doctor lumbered away. Sarah saw him move across the yard and up to the missile. The Mummy or guard paid no attention. Sarah guessed the intelligence of the Mummies was limited and strictly functional. They would do what they were ordered, no less, but no more. And since no one had actually told them to look out for another Mummy with a box of gelignite ... Sarah watched tensely as the Doctor made his way to the ramp. He climbed stiffly up it, and put the box just beside the open hatch. Sarah began lining up her rifle-sights. Now the Doctor was descending the ramp. He reached the bottom and started back towards her. Sarah cuddled the rifle-butt into her shoulder. Just let him get a little further from the missile and ... To her horror, she saw Marcus Scarman appear from the house and make straight for the Doctor.

Through a tiny gap in the wrappings the Doctor saw Scarman coming towards him, a white cylinder in his hands. He heard Scarman's voice. 'Stop!'

The Doctor went on walking. The voice came again. 'Stop! Turn about.'

The Doctor stopped, turned. Marcus came up to him. 'Is your relay defective?'

The Doctor stood motionless. Scarman frowned for a moment then held out the metal cylinder. 'This is the co-ordinate-selector. It is to be placed in the projection-dome monitor. Indicate your understanding.' The Doctor managed a Mummy-like nod.

'Then obey my order,' said Scarman sharply.

Stiffly the Doctor turned and reascended the ramp. Marcus moved back towards the house. Inside the rocket, the Doctor dumped the cylinder at random, and hurried back down the ramp.

Sarah watched impatiently as for the second time the

Doctor began walking across the yard towards her. This time there was no interruption. The Doctor maintained his stiff Mummy-like gait until the sentinel robot turned away from him, then he broke into a shambling run.

When he was near the edge of the trees, Sarah lined up her sights on the cardboard box. Slowly and carefully she squeezed the trigger ...

9

In the Power of Sutekh

The rifle cracked, and the butt recoiled against her shoulder. Sarah saw the cardboard box jerk. There was a sheet of flame then—nothing. No sound, and no explosion.

Sarah looked up as the disguised Doctor threw himself down beside her. 'I hit it, Doctor,' she said helplessly. 'I *know* I hit it!'

'You hit it all right,' agreed the Doctor grimly. 'Sutekh must be containing the explosion by sheer mental power. There's only one hope left, I've got to get to him. Somehow I've got to break his concentration.' Swiftly the Doctor began stripping off his Mummy disguise.

'Come on, Sarah,' he said urgently. 'Give me a hand.'

Sarah helped him to strip off the bindings. They rolled them into a ball and stuffed them under a bush. From beneath another bush the Doctor produced his hat, coat and scarf.

'He'll get himself killed over that silly hat and scarf one day,' thought Sarah, remembering how he'd gone back for his hat earlier.

Restored to his old self again, the Doctor stood up and stretched with evident relief. 'Somehow I don't think I was meant to be a Mummy,' he said solemnly. 'Anyway, I need to look my best to meet someone as distinguished as old Sutekh . . .'

Sarah was appalled. 'As distinguished as who? Doctor, you're not going down that Space/Time tunnel thing!'

'Oh yes I am, Sarah. If I can distract Sutekh for just one second, his concentration will break and the balloon, or rather the missile, will go up. Sutekh will be imprisoned again for ever. We'll have won!'

'Oh will we? We'll have won, and you'll be in Sutekh's den. How do you think he'll feel when he realises he's got you to thank for blowing up his missile and spoiling his plans for a comeback?'

'Well, he may be a bit put out,' the Doctor admitted, 'but I'm sure I'll manage to smooth him over.'

'And if you don't?'

'Then I'll just have to escape. After all, I've walked into many a tight spot before.'

'As tight as this?'

'Well, perhaps not quite as tight as this. Good-bye, Sarah.' He touched her cheek gently with his hand, turned and ran towards the front of the house.

Sarah called after him. 'Doctor, he'll kill you ...' But she was too late. The Doctor was gone. Dejected she turned back towards the Lodge for a hiding place. Her anxiety for the Doctor made her careless. Within minutes she ran straight into the arms of a Mummy. Seizing her arm in an iron grip, ignoring her cries and struggles, the Mummy started dragging her towards the Priory.

The organ note boomed out from the Casket. Marcus Scarman ran to stand before it.

'I hear you, Master,' he called.

'On the missile loading-ramp ... a crude detonation device. Another human attempt to delay my return. They must be found and punished—but first attend to the device. I cannot hold back the exothermic reaction for many minutes. It is taking an intense toll of ... available energy.' There was the sound of hideous strain in Sutekh's voice.

'It will be done immediately, Master.' Scarman bowed, and ran from the room.

The window opened and the Doctor clambered through. He moved cautiously over to the Casket, examined it for a moment, then touched a control inside it.

The Space/Time tunnel appeared. The Doctor stepped into it and was whirled away, spinning off into the depths of infinity. His senses blurred and he lost consciousness ...

So small and inconspicuous was the cardboard box that it took Marcus a moment or two to find it. He saw it at last, and ordered one of the Servicer robots forward. Stiffly it began walking up the ramp.

The Doctor recovered consciousness with a jolt, and found himself standing in the antechamber of an Egyptian tomb. A tapestry-covered doorway lay just before him. The Doctor reached out and moved the tapestry aside. It smouldered as he touched it, and he snatched back his hand. He paused for a moment, then bracing himself, stepped through the doorway.

He found himself in a dark, cave-like chamber. The Doctor had a quick impression of monitor screens and some kind of advanced computer. Dominating the chamber was the figure of Sutekh himself. He sat on a raised throne, a robed, masked figure, staring intently into a monitor. The screen showed a wavering picture of the pyramid-shaped missile, far away in England.

The Doctor drew a deep breath. Then he spoke, his voice deliberately loud and resonant. 'Greetings, Sutekh, last of the Osirians!'

Slowly Sutekh turned his head, his concentration momentarily broken ...

On the missile ramp the Mummy bent to pick up the box ... There was the sudden roar of an explosion. Mummy and missile disappeared in a sheet of flame.

Sutekh's head swung back to the monitor screen. Appalled, he watched the destruction of the missile that represented his only chance of freedom. The masked head turned slowly to the Doctor and a blaze of fierce green light burned from its eyes. As the light struck him, the Doctor was transfixed, helpless, writhing in agony ...

For a long moment Sutekh watched the Doctor's suffering. Then the glow faded from his eyes, and he spoke in a voice of restrained fury. 'No ... you shall not die yet. Death would be too easy. Identify yourself.'

The Doctor's voice was scarcely more than a painful

whisper. 'Destroy me, Sutekh. Enjoy your revenge. Nothing else is left within your power.'

'Identify yourself!' Sutekh's eyes glowed once more, and again the Doctor writhed in agony. 'It is in my power to choose the manner of your death,' said the hateful voice. 'I can if I choose, keep you alive for centuries, wracked by the most excruciating pain. Since it is your interference that has condemned me to remain for ever prisoner of the Eye of Horus, that would be a fitting end for you. You might make an amusing diversion.' The green light died down. 'Identify yourself—plaything of Sutekh,' said the voice contemptuously.

The Doctor gasped weakly. 'I am a ... traveller ...'

'From where?'

'Gallifrey, in the Constellation of Kasteroborous.'

'These names mean nothing to me,' snarled Sutekh. 'What is the binary location from galactic zero centre?'

Now that he was free of the incessant pain, some of the Doctor's strength was returning to him. His voice was firmer as he replied. 'Ten, zero eleven ... zero ... zero ... by zero two.'

Sutekh considered. 'It seems to me that I know this planet.' He looked towards the computer and ordered, 'Data retrieval.' On a screen numbers and hieroglyphics appeared, changing swiftly, fixing at last on a single line of complex symbols. There was a ring of triumph in Sutekh's voice. 'So! You are a Time Lord!'

The Doctor shook his head. 'Not in the sense that you mean; I come of the Time Lord race, but I renounced their society. Now I am simply a traveller.'

'A traveller in Time and Space?' asked Sutekh eagerly.

The Doctor did not reply.

'In Time and Space?' Sutekh insisted.

Reluctantly the Doctor nodded. Sutekh's voice dropped almost to a whisper. 'Approach closer.' Reluctantly the Doctor moved nearer the throne. 'What are you called, Time Lord?'

'I am called the Doctor.'

'I offer you an alliance, Doctor. Serve me truly and an empire can be yours.'

The Doctor drew back. 'Serve *you*, Sutekh? Your name is abomination in every civilised world. Whether that name be Set, Satan, Sadok ...'

The voice of Sutekh hardened. 'You *shall* serve me, Doctor ...'

'Never.' The Doctor's voice was utterly determined.

The green glow blazed out from the eye-slits of Sutekh's mask. Caught in its beam, the Doctor twisted in agony.

Sutekh laughed. 'You dare to pit your puny will against mine? Kneel ! Kneel before the might of Sutekh.'

Slowly, fighting the power of Sutekh's mind every inch of the way, the Doctor was forced to his knees. Sutekh's voice boomed out. 'In my presence you are an ant, a worm, a termite. Abase yourself, you grovelling insect.'

The booming note of the organ-signal interrupted Sutekh's sport. The face of Marcus Scarman appeared on a monitor screen 'Well?' demanded Sutekh. 'Speak!'

'Sutekh, great master, a Servicer has captured one of the humans responsible for the destruction of your missile.'

Sutekh said dismissively. 'The extra-terrestial, their leader, is already my prisoner. I have no interest in the other humans.'

Scarman waved the Mummy forward. 'Then this prisoner can be destroyed?' To his horror, the Doctor saw Sarah struggling in the Mummy's grip.

Sutekh nodded indifferently. 'Let it be killed at once.'

The Doctor struggled to his feet. 'No, Sutekh!'

On the monitor he saw the Mummy holding Sarah grasp her more firmly, while another raised its great hand for the death blow ...

'No!' he shouted again.

Suddenly Sutekh intervened. 'Wait! Keep the human alive, Scarman. It may yet have some use.'

'As you command, Great One.' Marcus raised his hand in a signal and the Mummies became motionless once more.

Sutekh turned to the Doctor. 'You are a Time Lord. What interest have you in humans?'

The Doctor knew what would happen if he admitted that Sarah's fate was important to him. 'I have long taken an interest in Earth and human beings,' he said calmly. 'All sapient life-forms are our kin, Sutekh.'

Angrily Sutekh hissed. 'Horus held that view—but I refute it. All life is my enemy.'

'And I know why,' said the Doctor boldly. 'Because you fear them. You fear that some other intelligent life-form will arise, and grow to rival you in power. So you destroy all life, wherever you find it.'

By deliberately provoking Sutekh, the Doctor hoped to divert his attention away from Sarah. Sutekh's next words made him realise that the attempt had failed.

'Your words are a cloud,' said Sutekh slowly. 'But I see through them, and into your mind.' The green eyes behind the mask-slits burned into the Doctor's own. 'The human girl ... ah, I see. She travels with you, Doctor, does she not, in this—TARDIS?'

Sutekh looked towards his monitor screen. Slowly an image of the TARDIS began to form. The Doctor's shoulders slumped defeatedly. 'If you read *my* mind by mental force, Sutekh, then nothing can be beyond you.'

A note of self-pity crept into Sutekh's voice. 'Nothing. Except to free myself from this prison in which Horus has bound me.'

'Your imprisonment was well deserved,' said the Doctor sternly. 'You chose to use your great powers for evil.'

Again Sutekh gave his chilling laugh. 'Your evil is my good, Doctor. I am Sutekh the Destroyer. Where I tread I leave nothing but dust and darkness. *That* I find good.'

The Doctor straightened up. 'Then I curse you in the name of all nature, Sutekh. You are a twisted abhorrence.'

The eye-slits in Sutekh's mask blazed green. A cry of pain was torn from the Doctor's lips as the ray caught him with all its agonising force. Through a roaring in his ears he heard the cold voice of Sutekh. 'Any further insolence, Doctor, and I shall shred your nervous system into a million fibres. Is it understood?'

The green light faded and the Doctor dropped to the ground, almost unconscious. For a moment Sutekh sat considering the crumpled figure. The key of the TARDIS rose on its chain around the Doctor's neck. The loop of the chain pulled itself over his head and floated in the air, propelled by the power of Sutekh's will.

The recovering Doctor looked on helplessly as the key floated before Sutekh's mask. Then Sutekh called, 'Scarman!'

Immediately Marcus's face appeared on the monitor. 'I hear you, Master.'

'See,' said Sutekh exultantly. 'My enemies have brought me my deliverance. The Doctor's TARDIS will be the means of my escape!'

10

A Journey to Mars

Gripped firmly by the Mummy, Sarah saw a tiny object appear, far down the Space/Time tunnel. It grew larger and larger until it shot out of the Casket, and dropped into Marcus Scarman's hands.

Sarah gasped in horror. 'The TARDIS key!' Now she knew that the Doctor was a helpless prisoner in Sutekh's hands. He would never otherwise have parted with the TARDIS key.

Sarah heard the voice of Sutekh boom out from the glowing green casket. 'This allows you entry to the Time Lord's Time/Space machine. Take one Servicer, and travel to the Pyramids of Mars.'

In Sutekh's cell, the Doctor was struggling to his feet. Despite all he had undergone, a little of his old jauntiness was returning. 'I'm afraid Scarman won't find it possible to obey your order, Sutekh.'

The masked figure glared down at him. 'Marcus Scarman is my puppet. My mind is in his.'

The Doctor managed a smile. 'Perhaps so. But the controls of the TARDIS are isomorphic.'

'One to one ...' mused Sutekh. 'I see. So they will answer to you alone?'

'Correct.'

'Then it seems I was wise to spare you, Doctor. Scarman!'

In the Egyptian room, Marcus Scarman, the

TARDIS key in his hand, turned back to the Casket. Sutekh's voice rolled out triumphantly. 'I send you my captive. The Time Lord will control the machine. The human girl will accompany you. If the Time Lord attempts treachery, kill her.'

Marcus bowed. 'It is understood, Master.'

Sarah strained her eyes to look into the Space/Time tunnel. Again she saw a tiny shape spinning towards them. As it grew larger, it turned into the Doctor, sitting cross-legged like a Buddhist monk in meditation. The figure grew life-size, straightened up and emerged from the mouth of the Casket. The Doctor stood quite motionless, while the Space/Time tunnel glow faded behind him.

Wrenching free from the grip of the Mummy, Sarah tried to run to him. Marcus thrust out an arm and barred her way. 'Stand back. He is possessed by the Great One.'

Sarah called, 'Doctor, it's me!' The Doctor made no reply. He was staring straight ahead, his face completely blank.

Marcus stepped in front of him. 'Whom do you serve, Time Lord?'

For a moment the Doctor was silent. Then his lips moved and a single word came from his mouth. 'Sutekh.'

'Who holds all life in his hands?'

'Sutekh.'

'Who is the bringer of death?'

'Sutekh.'

Scarman nodded satisfied. 'Venerate his name, and obey him in all things.'

One final sentence seemed forced from the Doctor's lips. 'Sutekh is supreme.'

Sadly Sarah whispered, 'Oh, Doctor ...' It was terrible to see the Doctor, always so independent, reduced to a mindless puppet, parroting praise of Sutekh.

Marcus was speaking to the Casket. 'Control is established, Great One.'

'It is well,' said Sutekh's voice. 'But these Time Lords are a cunning and perfidious species. Dispose of him when you reach the Pyramids of Mars.'

'It shall be done, Sutekh.' He turned to the Doctor. 'Come.'

The Doctor followed Scarman out of the room.

Before Sarah could protest, the Mummy dragged her after them.

In the Egyptian room, Scarman handed the key to the Doctor, who opened the TARDIS doors and led the way inside. He went straight to the controls, closed the door and set the TARDIS in motion.

Marcus Scarman and the Mummy stood motionless, showing no reaction as the take-off noise began and the central column began to rise and fall. Sarah managed to move closer to the control column. 'Doctor, it's me, Sarah,' she hissed again. The Doctor ignored her, moving blank-faced around the console.

The nightmare journey was soon over. The Doctor landed the TARDIS, opened the doors and went out. Marcus, Sarah and the Mummy followed. The Doctor closed the door and stood waiting.

Sarah looked around her. She was in a huge stone chamber, which might have been the interior of a pyramid somewhere on Earth. The strangest thing about the place was the fact that it seemed to have no entrance or exit. Every wall was a blank face of solid stone.

Marcus walked across to the nearest wall. The voice of Sutekh, distant but still clear, echoed through the chamber. 'My reading indicates that you are in an antechamber under the main Pyramid. Seek the control centre. Scan for the door.'

Marcus stretched out a hand, and swept it to and fro across the stone. His hands traced the outline of a door —and a door appeared. Marcus was about to step through it, then he turned. 'Sutekh has no further need of the Time Lord. Destroy him.'

Sarah screamed, 'No!' and threw herself in front of the Doctor. The Mummy swept her aside with one savage blow, and she reeled against the far wall. The Mummy locked its huge hands round the Doctor's throat and squeezed. The Doctor stood motionless, making no attempt to defend himself. Its gruesome work done, the Mummy let go and stepped back. The Doctor's body dropped limply to the floor.

'Come,' said Marcus impatiently. He stepped through the door, the Mummy lumbering behind him.

Sarah got to her knees and crawled painfully across to the Doctor. She wondered why they hadn't killed her too. Perhaps she just wasn't important enough ... She'd die here anyway in time. Or perhaps Sutekh himself would blast her once he was free. Such was Sarah's misery that her own fate hardly interested her. She fell across the Doctor's body, sobbing bitterly, thinking only of the way he'd been savagely murdered before her eyes ...

A hand tapped her on the shoulder and a muffled voice said reprovingly, 'Sarah, you're soaking my shirt!'

Incredulously, she realised that both hand and voice belonged to the Doctor. She sat up and looked at him. 'Doctor, you're alive.'

The Doctor sat up too, rubbing his neck and wincing. 'Well, of course I'm alive. Respiratory bypass system. Very useful in a tight squeeze. Mind you, I'll have a bit of a stiff neck for a while.'

'I thought you'd been turned into another zombie, like Scarman.'

The Doctor rose, helping Sarah to her feet. 'Well, I suppose I must have been for a while. But once Sutekh didn't need me any more he stopped thinking about me. His mind relaxed its grip.' He looked round interestedly. 'Now then, where are we?'

'Sutekh ordered you to take us to the Pyramids of Mars. Marcus and one of the Mummies came with us.'

'Yes, of course. Sutekh will have sent Marcus here to deactivate the forcefield control in the Pyramid. Which way did he go?'

'Through that door,' gasped Sarah. 'Well, there *was* a door. It seems to have vanished.' The stone wall was blank and smooth again.

The Doctor studied the area of wall. 'A door can't vanish,' he said severely. 'That simply isn't logical. It's just that the door isn't visible.'

Sarah shrugged. 'Same difference, surely.'

The Doctor was examining the wall with feverish

intensity. 'I've got to find Marcus ... Somehow I've got to stop him.'

Marcus Scarman, the Servicer robot behind him, was patiently walking along an endless stone passage. He halted only when a blank metal wall barred his way. Just to one side of it was a switch. Marcus reached out to touch it, but the voice of Sutekh warned, 'Stop. I sense danger. That relay switch is a power conductor terminal. The true bulkhead release will be concealed. Scan!'

Again Marcus stretched out his hand and moved it over the surface of the metal bulkhead. 'There—now!' said Sutekh exultantly. Marcus touched the indicated point and a small panel swung open to reveal a switch. He operated it, the bulkhead slid back and Marcus went on his way, the Mummy following behind.

The Doctor was tracing his fingers over the chamber wall, just as Marcus had done before him. He found the right area at last, and the door reappeared beneath his hand. 'Triobyphysics,' said the Doctor in a pleased tone, and led the way through.

They followed the stone passage and came to the same metal wall that had blocked Marcus's progress. The Doctor reached for the switch, then drew back his hand.

'What's the matter?' asked Sarah.

'Too obvious—and too easy.'

'A door handle usually is obvious, surely?'

'Not in a jail,' said the Doctor. 'Horus would have left traps for the unwary intruder.'

'I thought Horus was one of the good guys?'

'He was an Osirian—with all their guile and ingenuity.' The Doctor was studying the metal door as he spoke. 'They had dome-shaped heads and cerebrums like spiral staircases. They just couldn't help being devious!'

The Doctor's searching fingers found the hidden panel. It sprung open to reveal the second switch. The Doctor operated it and the wall slid back. He turned to Sarah and grinned, childishly, pleased with his own cleverness. They went on their way, the wall sliding back behind them.

There followed a long journey through more and more passages. Frustratingly it ended before yet another bulkhead, exactly like the previous one.

'Maybe we've come in a circle?' suggested Sarah.

The Doctor shook his head. 'This one is similar— but not the same.' He looked at the wall switch, then opened the hidden panel. As he was reaching for the panel switch he drew back his hand. 'Now, Horus wouldn't set exactly the same trap a second time—or would he?' The Doctor stood brooding. 'I wonder. Double or triple bluff.'

Sarah pointed to the wall switch. 'You mean Horus might expect a visitor to work out that the panel switch would be booby-trapped—and still booby-trap this one?'

The Doctor rubbed his chin. 'Or if Horus expected an intruder to work that out, he might booby-trap the panel switch anyway!'

'So what do we do?'

'We apply scientific method, Sarah. We test our suspicions.' The Doctor produced an extendable electronic probe and swept its end across the panel switch. There was a bang and a flash. The probe flew from his hand as the panel switch exploded in sparks and smoke. The Doctor sucked his fingers, recovered the probe and operated the wall switch. The barrier slid back. 'Triple bluff,' said the Doctor happily, and they went on their way.

Some way ahead of them Marcus Scarman was confronting yet another metal wall, this one studded with several rows of switches.

'Stand back and scan,' ordered Sutekh. Marcus stood back, sweeping his hand backwards and forwards across the wall.

On Earth, in Sutekh's Egyptian cell, the wall appeared on a monitor screen as a pattern of dots joined by radiating lines, with rows of binary numbers superimposed. Sutekh laughed. 'Horus, do you think to confound Sutekh with these childish stratagems?'

On Mars, Marcus heard the familiar voice. 'The floor is charged with explosive. Count to the fifth row up—now, the extreme right switch.'

The bulkhead slid back, and Marcus went through. The Mummy followed him. It paused for a moment, looking back suspiciously. Then it followed Marcus and the bulkhead slid closed behind it.

Seconds later, the Doctor's and Sarah's heads popped round the corner. 'That was a near one,' whispered

Sarah. 'I thought it had seen us.' She looked at the wall. 'Oh Doctor, there are dozens of switches.'

The Doctor pointed to an immensely complicated graph on the wall to one side of the bulkhead. 'Horus has very kindly provided a key, though.'

'Some key,' muttered Sarah. 'What does it mean?'

The Doctor had fished out a grubby scrap of paper and a stub of pencil. 'Well, obviously the length of the lines provides a scale of measurements.'

Sarah studied the graph, shaking her head. 'Didn't you run into something like this in the City of the Exxilons?'

The Doctor was in no mood to discuss his past adventures, particularly those which had taken place in earlier incarnations. He was muttering busily to himself. He looked up as Sarah stretched out a tentative hand to one of the switches, half inclined to choose by good old feminine intuition.

'Don't touch anything,' he said sharply.

Sarah snatched back her hand. 'I wasn't going to.'

'Well, don't. One false move and you'll probably set off an explosive charge!'

The Doctor returned to his calculations. 'Now let me see. Twenty point three centimetres multiplied by the binary figure ten zero zero ... that's a pretty simple calculation ...'

'Show off!' muttered Sarah rather sulkily.

The Doctor ignored her. He whipped off his scarf and held it before him like a tape-measure. 'Now then, feet and inches one side, metres and centimetres the other. One hundred and sixty-two point four—that should be about three stitches.'

The Doctor made a few measurements, then slung his scarf back round his neck. He muttered more calculations, all totally incomprehensible to Sarah, and stretched out his hand. 'Now I *think* this is the right switch ...'

Nervously Sarah asked, 'What happens if you're wrong?'

'I imagine we'll all be blown to blazes,' said the Doctor cheerfully. He reached out and flicked the switch.

II

The Guardians of Horus

Instinctively Sarah drew back from the bulkhead. For a moment after the Doctor pressed the switch—the extreme right-hand switch on the fifth row up—nothing happened. Then the bulkhead drew slowly back. The Doctor gave Sarah a self-satisfied smile and walked through. Sarah followed and the door closed behind them. They found themselves in a dark chamber, lit only by strangely-glowing walls. They moved forward cautiously, almost feeling their way. Sarah stopped and looked up at the Doctor. 'Which way do we go now?'

'I'm not too sure. Stay here, while I look around.' The Doctor moved on a few paces. There came a sudden scream from Sarah, just as suddenly cut off by a hollow, ringing sound. The Doctor whirled round. Sarah was trapped inside a transparent glass bell. She hammered frantically at the glass, her lips moving soundlessly.

The Doctor moved round the bell, studying it. 'A Decatron crucible,' he muttered to himself. There was no way to break into it—it would have to be removed by the agency which had placed it there. Unless it *was* removed, and quickly, Sarah was going to die of suffocation. 'All right, Sarah, keep calm,' called the Doctor, although he knew she couldn't hear him.

Inside the bell, Sarah was shouting frantically. The

Doctor sighed. 'Oh, Sarah, I should never have brought you here.' Then he lip-read her words.

'Look out. Behind you.'

The Doctor spun round. Two Mummies had materialised in the darkness. They were similar to the robot servants of Sutekh, but larger, and the golden ornamentation of their bindings seemed to suggest some kind of rank.

A voice spoke out of the darkness. It was like and yet unlike that of Sutekh, its tones holding wisdom and power rather than Sutekh's cruelty and hatred. 'Intruders,' the great voice boomed, 'you face the twin guardians of Horus. One is programmed to deceive, the other points truly. These two switches control your fate—instant freedom, or instant death.'

A section of wall with two switches set into it was suddenly illuminated.

The Doctor walked over to the switches and stood before them.

The voice said, 'Before you choose you can ask *one* guardian *one* question. This is the riddle of the Osirians. Which is the guardian of life?'

The Doctor's mind was racing frantically. He glanced across at Sarah, already showing signs of distress inside the glass bell. Unless he solved the riddle soon she was doomed. He looked again at the two impassive figures of the Mummies. 'Which indeed,' he thought. 'Now if they're contra-programmed, so one *must* always give a false indication ...'

The Doctor smiled. He turned to the nearest guardian. 'One question, eh? Now, if I were to ask your chum there, your fellow guardian, which was the switch that meant life—which one would he indicate?'

The guardian swung round and pointed to the switch on the Doctor's right. The Doctor nodded. 'I see. So if you're the true guardian, that must be the death switch. And if you're the automatic liar, you're trying to deceive me. So that must still be the death switch.' Hoping his logic was water-tight, the Doctor pulled the switch on his left. The two guardians disappeared—and so did the glass bell surrounding Sarah. Gasping for breath she staggered out into the Doctor's arms. He steadied her on her feet. 'Are you all right?' She nodded weakly. 'Then come on. We've got no time to lose.'

In his cell on Earth, an impatient Sutekh was following the progress of his servants through the Martian Pyramid. On the monitor Sutekh could see a squat, tomb-like shape. 'The inner chamber,' he hissed. 'The control centre of the Pyramids! The sign of the Eye, Scarman. Make the sign of the Eye!'

On Mars, standing before the door of the tomb, Scarman sketched the sign of the Eye with one hand. There was a high-pitched electronic sound and the door swung open. Behind it was blackness. Marcus Scarman moved slowly inside.

He found himself in a chamber of light, lit by a flickering eerie glow from walls and floor. In the centre of the chamber cradled in a silver tulip-shaped cup was what appeared to be a giant ruby, bigger than a man's head. Four silver rods projected from it, like the rays of a stylised sun, and it pulsated regularly with a fierce red glow.

Scarman heard the exultant voice of Sutekh. 'It is the Eye. The Eye of Horus. Destroy! Destroy! Destroy!'

Scarman moved towards the Eye. A huge Mummy stepped from the darkness, wearing the gold ornamented bands that denoted the guardians of Horus. Marcus said sharply, 'Stop. Deactivate!' The guardian came on.

From the air a voice spoke. 'The servants of Horus obey only the voice of Horus.' Its tone changed. 'Drive out these intruders.'

Marcus dropped back, and waved his own Mummy forward. 'Attack!'

The two giant figures lumbered towards each other, colliding with a mighty impact in the centre of the chamber. They began to attack each other with great swinging blows. As the two giants battled on, Marcus Scarman was able to move closer to the Eye. He stretched out his hands, hearing the voice of Sutekh. 'Destroy! Destroy! Destroy!'

Marcus Scarman's whole body seemed to blaze with energy, as he became the channel for Sutekh's powers. The Doctor and Sarah ran through the open door and skidded to a halt. The figure before the Eye had the body of Marcus Scarman. But its head was that of Sutekh. Not the savage mask that the Doctor had already seen, but Sutekh's true visage, the snarling, bestial, jackal face that had appeared to Sarah in the TARDIS.

For a moment they stood frozen in horror, and that

moment was all Sutekh needed. Mental energy poured through Marcus Scarman, and the Eye of Horus exploded in a shattering blast.

Sutekh's head faded and Marcus, once again in his own form, swung round to face the Doctor. But it was still the exultant voice of Sutekh that came from his lips. 'Free! I am free at last!'

The body of Marcus Scarman collapsed, disintegrating before their eyes into a heap of smoking ashes.

In an awe-stricken voice Sarah whispered, 'He's won. Sutekh's won!'

The Doctor stood quite still. The Chamber was silent.

The two Mummies had battered each other into mutual destruction. Still locked together in conflict, they lay motionless on the floor.

Suddenly the Doctor's face lit up. 'Not yet, he hasn't,' he shouted. 'He's forgotten the Time Factor. Come on, Sarah—*run!*'

Exultantly Sutekh looked round his cell for the last time. 'I have won my freedom, Horus,' he roared. 'Now begins the reign of Sutekh the Destroyer. I shall crush this miserable planet Earth and hurl it into the outermost depths of space. My vengeance starts here!'

The Weapon of the Time Lords

The Doctor and Sarah covered the distance from the Chamber of the Eye back to the TARDIS in a single mad dash. Doors opened and closed before them as though the Pyramid of Horus itself was co-operating with their flight. The Doctor's speed was such that Sarah could scarcely keep up with him. By the time she reached the TARDIS, the Doctor was already inside. The control column was moving up and down, the dematerialisation noise filling the air.

With a shriek of 'Wait for me!' Sarah leaped through the TARDIS doors just as they closed.

The Doctor was working feverishly as the TARDIS made the journey back to the Earth of nineteen eleven. He had already removed a side panel from the TARDIS console by the time they landed. The instant the centre column stopped moving the Doctor began to dismantle part of the TARDIS's control console. He extracted a complex piece of equipment and ran out of the TARDIS at top speed, wires trailing behind him. Sarah followed, wondering what was happening but not daring to ask. It was clear from the Doctor's manner that even a second's delay could be fatal.

Stiffly, Sutekh rose from his throne and took a step forward. 'The paralysis has left me,' he said exultantly. 'I can move again, I can move!'

He threw both arms wide in a gesture of triumph. 'Now, Horus, we shall see who rules the cosmos!'

In the organ room, the Doctor knelt by the Casket, working at frantic speed. He was attaching the trailing wires from the piece of TARDIS machinery to the Casket's control panel. His fingers moved in a blur of activity.

As he made the last connection, he looked up and smiled, seeming to notice Sarah for the first time. 'According to my estimate, we've got about twenty seconds,' he said calmly.

'Twenty seconds to what?' wondered Sarah. Suddenly the Space/Time tunnel effect began building up in the mouth of the Casket. The Doctor smiled. 'Well, here he comes,' he said. 'Right on time!' He might have been talking about an Inter-City Express.

A tiny speck had appeared in the depths of the endless tunnel. It came closer and closer, then turned into the terrifying figure of Sutekh. His mask was gone, and the jackal head snarled savagely at them.

When the figure reached the mouth of the Casket it seemed to pause and hover. 'Who is here?' demanded Sutekh hoarsely. 'Who dares to interfere with my vengeance?'

The Doctor stepped boldly forward. 'I do, Sutekh. You forgot that Time is the weapon of the Time Lords. I have used Time to defeat you. You are caught in a Temporal trap.'

Sutekh gave a scream of rage. 'Time Lord, I shall

destroy you. I shall destroy you . . .'

His voice faded and diminished, as the Doctor spun one of the controls on his TARDIS equipment. At once Sutekh dwindled, retreating down the tunnel, his voice fading away. The Doctor spun more dials, and Sutekh moved forward, hovering, trapped at the mouth of the Casket.

The Doctor looked dispassionately at him. 'How long do Osirians live, Sutekh?'

The Doctor adjusted more dials, and once again the figure of Sutekh retreated slowly down the endless Space/Time tunnel. 'Release me,' he screamed.

'Never! You're trapped again, Sutekh, trapped in the corridor of eternity.'

The voice of the dwindling figure floated back down the tunnel. 'Release me, insect, or I shall destroy the cosmos.'

The Doctor shook his head. 'You're a thousand years past the twentieth century, Sutekh. Go on for another ten thousand.' His face set and remorseless, the Doctor spun another dial.

Faintly the voice called, 'Release me and I will spare the planet Earth. I'll give it to you for a plaything. Release me! Release me . . . Release me . . .'

The Doctor shouted, 'No, Sutekh, the time of the Osirians is long past. Go *on*!' The Doctor gave the dial a final turn and stepped back. From far down the tunnel came the death scream of Sutekh, fading away into eternal nothingness.

The Doctor heaved a great sigh of relief. 'That's it, Sarah. All over. He lived about another seven thousand years.'

Sarah could hardly believe it. 'He's dead? Sutekh is really dead?'

'At last.' The Doctor began unclipping the leads joining the section of the console to the Casket.

Sarah perched on a chair and watched him. 'I know that's the Time Control Unit from the TARDIS. But what did you actually do with it?'

'I moved the threshold of the Space/Time tunnel into the far future, so Sutekh could never reach the end.'

'But Sutekh was free! How were you able to——'

The Doctor beamed. 'Elementary, my dear Sarah. After the Eye of Horus was destroyed, I realised we still had just over two minutes to get back here and deal with Sutekh—the time it takes radio waves to pass from Mars to Earth.'

Suddenly Sarah understood. 'So the Eye of Horus was *still* holding Sutekh—for two minutes after it was broken?'

Unclipping the last of his leads, the Doctor got wearily to his feet. He stared for a moment down the endless Space/Time tunnel, as if still seeing the dwindling figure of Sutekh. 'The Egyptians called him the Typhonian Beast, you know,' he said absently.

Before Sarah could reply, there was an explosion inside the Casket. Smoke and flames began belching out from its mouth.

The Doctor gave a contrite tut-tut. 'Now that *was* careless of me. I should have realised the thermal balance would equalise ...'

The Casket had turned into a furnace, lashing out sheets of flame. Interestedly the Doctor moved over to investigate, but Sarah pulled him back. 'Doctor, you remember the Old Priory was burned to the ground?'

The Doctor looked thoughtful. 'Yes, maybe it *is* time we were getting out of here. Don't want to get the blame for starting a fire, do we?'

Sarah had a nightmare vision of trying to explain recent happenings at the Priory to some heavily-moustached village policeman of the year nineteen eleven. 'Oh no,' she said fervently, 'we don't want that.'

They ran out of the Organ room, along the corridors and back towards the Egyptian room. The fire was spreading with amazing rapidity and they had to make a desperate dash for the TARDIS through smoke and flames.

Once they were inside, the Doctor closed the door, shutting off the roar of the flames. Working quickly he wired the Time Control Unit back into the centre console and closed the panel. He touched controls and the dematerialisation noise began.

Outside the TARDIS, the Egyptian room was an inferno. The blazing roof collapsed in flames, just as the TARDIS disappeared.

The fire spread rapidly through the old house. Walls began to collapse and the roof fell in. The woods around the house caught, and the fire even spread to the Lodge. Soon most of the Scarman estate was an inferno of flame.

Safe inside the TARDIS, Sarah waited for it to return her to her own time. The Doctor was quietly checking over the instrument console, showing little sign of his recent ordeal. Sarah, weary and exhausted, wanted only to return to familiar twentieth-century surroundings. She was still haunted by the death of Sutekh—and all the other deaths that had gone before. There had been so many ... The old servant, Collins. Ibrahim Namin, the servant of Sutekh, discarded when he was no longer needed. The bluff and hearty Doctor Warlock. Poor little Ernie Clements, the poacher. Laurence Scarman—she could remember him looking round the TARDIS with bright-eyed eagerness. And most tragic of all, Marcus Scarman, taken over and burnt out by Sutekh's horrible alien power. She remembered Sutekh free only briefly after his long captivity, screaming with powerless rage as he died in the Doctor's temporal trap.

'Doctor,' she asked, 'Won't all this business get out? I mean, *didn't* it get out, back in nineteen eleven? Everything that happened at the Old Priory?'

The Doctor looked up from the console. 'I very much doubt it, Sarah. Time has a way of taking care of these things. Anyway, when we get back home, you can look it up and see!'

Epilogue

Later, much later, when she finally arrived safely back on Earth after many adventures, Sarah remembered the Doctor's words. She went to the offices of the local paper in the little country town near UNIT H.Q. and persuaded them to let her see the files for nineteen eleven. Before long she found the item she wanted.

BROTHERS DIE IN TRAGIC FIRE
HOLOCAUST SWEEPS COUNTRY ESTATE
Many others feared killed.

The whole countryside was shocked and saddened to-day by the news of the tragic fire at the Old Priory in which a number of well-known local figures perished. Fire broke out suddenly during the night and swept the Priory, the Lodge and much of the heavily wooded estate at great speed.

Among the victims of the blaze is believed to be Professor Marcus Scarman, the well-known Egyptologist, who had just returned from a successful archaeological expedition to Egypt. His brother Laurence, the distinguished amateur scientist, also died in the flames. Further victims include Josiah Collins, who had been in the service of the Scarmans all his life, a Mr Ibrahim Namin, believed to have been a guest of

*Professor Scarman, and a family friend, Doctor War-
lock who was visiting the Priory. In the grounds, the
remains were discovered of Ernest Clements, a local
villager with a history of poaching. It is feared that this
unfortunate man was trapped by the blaze while en-
gaged in his nefarious pursuits.*

*An element of mystery still surrounds the death of
Professor Scarman himself. He had not been home for
some time, and was thought to be on his way back
from Cairo. However, investigations in Cairo revealed
that Professor Scarman had left some time ago. It is
believed that the unfortunate Professor, by an un-
lucky coincidence, must have returned to his ancestral
home on the very night of the fire, though as yet no
trace of his remains have been discovered.*

*The cause of the blaze is still unknown, but there is
speculation in the village that one of the many advanced scientific devices which Mr Laurence Scarman
had installed in the Lodge may somehow have been
responsible ...*

Sarah skimmed through the rest of the report. So that
was what the Doctor had meant. The terrible events
surrounding the return of Sutekh had found a natural
explanation, a deplorable but soon forgotten tragedy
in an English country village.

Sarah looked through the window, out into the bust-
ling high street of the little country town. She shivered
at the memory of the desolate world she had seen
through the doors of the TARDIS—the world Sutekh
would have made if he had not been defeated. The
sacrifice of all those lives had not been in vain. The

pity was that no one would ever know.

Sarah closed the heavy old volume and went into the summer sunshine of her own, unchanged, twentieth century.

'Doctor Who'

Δ	0426114558	Terrance Dicks **DOCTOR WHO AND THE ABOMINABLE SNOWMEN**	70p
Δ	0426200373	Terrance Dicks **DOCTOR WHO AND THE ANDROID INVASION**	60p
Δ	0426116313	Ian Marter **DOCTOR WHO AND THE ARK IN SPACE**	70p
Δ	0426116747	Terrance Dicks **DOCTOR WHO AND THE BRAIN OF MORBIUS**	60p
Δ	0426110250	Terrance Dicks **DOCTOR WHO AND THE CARNIVAL OF MONSTERS**	70p
Δ	042611471X	Malcolm Hulke **DOCTOR WHO AND THE CAVE-MONSTERS**	70p
Δ	0426117034	Terrance Dicks **DOCTOR WHO AND THE CLAWS OF AXOS**	70p
Δ	0426113160	David Whitaker **DOCTOR WHO AND THE CRUSADERS**	70p
Δ	0426114981	Brian Hayles **DOCTOR WHO AND THE CURSE OF PELADON**	70p
Δ	042611244X	Terrance Dicks **DOCTOR WHO AND THE DALEK INVASION OF EARTH**	70p
Δ	0426103807	Terrance Dicks **DOCTOR WHO AND THE DAY OF THE DALEKS**	70p
Δ	0426101103	David Whitaker * **DOCTOR WHO AND THE DALEKS**	70p
Δ	0426119657	Terrance Dicks **DOCTOR WHO AND THE DEADLY ASSASSIN**	60p
Δ	0426200063	Terrance Dicks **DOCTOR WHO AND THE FACE OF EVIL**	70p
Δ	0426112601	Terrance Dicks **DOCTOR WHO AND THE GENESIS OF THE DALEKS**	60p

† For sale in Britain and Ireland only.
* Not for sale in Canada.
♦ Film & T.V. tie-ins.

Δ	0426118936	Philip Hinchcliffe **DOCTOR WHO AND THE** **MASQUE OF MANDRAGORA**	**70p**
Δ	0426112520	Terrance Dicks **DOCTOR WHO AND THE** **PLANET OF THE DALEKS**	**60p**
Δ	0426106555	Terrance Dicks **DOCTOR WHO AND THE PLANET OF** **THE SPIDERS**	**70p**
Δ	0426200616	Terrance Dicks **DOCTOR WHO AND THE** **ROBOTS OF DEATH**	**70p**
Δ	042611308X	Malcolm Hulke **DOCTOR WHO AND THE** **SEA-DEVILS**	**70p**
Δ	0426116585	Philip Hinchcliffe **DOCTOR WHO AND THE** **SEEDS OF DOOM**	**60p**
Δ	0426200497	Ian Marter **DOCTOR WHO AND THE** **SONTARAN EXPERIMENT**	**60p**
Δ	0426110331	Malcolm Hulke **DOCTOR WHO AND THE** **SPACE WAR**	**60p**
Δ	0426119738	Terrance Dicks **DOCTOR WHO AND THE** **TALONS OF WENG-CHIANG**	**60p**
Δ	0426115007	Terrance Dicks **DOCTOR WHO AND THE** **TERROR OF THE AUTONS**	**60p**
Δ	0426200233	Terrance Dicks **DOCTOR WHO AND THE** **TIME WARRIOR**	**60p**
Δ	0426113241	Bill Strutton **DOCTOR WHO AND THE ZARBI (illus)**	**70p**
Δ	0426200012	Terrance Dicks **THE SECOND DOCTOR WHO** **MONSTER BOOK (Colour illus)**	**70p**
	0426118421	Terrance Dicks **DOCTOR WHO DINOSAUR BOOK**	**75p**
	0426116151	Terrance Dicks and Malcolm Hulke **THE MAKING OF DOCTOR WHO**	**60p**
	0426200020	**DOCTOR WHO DISCOVERS** **PREHISTORIC ANIMALS (NF) (illus)**	**75p**

†For sale in Britain and Ireland only.
*Not for sale in Canada.
♦ Film & T.V. tie-ins.

If you enjoyed this book and would like to have information sent to you about other TARGET titles, write to the address below.

You will also receive:
A FREE TARGET BADGE!
Based on the TARGET BOOKS symbol — see front cover of this book — this attractive three-colour badge, pinned to your blazer-lapel or jumper, will excite the interest and comment of all your friends!

and you will be further entitled to:
FREE ENTRY INTO THE TARGET DRAW!
All you have to do is cut off the coupon below, write on it your name and address in *block capitals,* and pin it to your letter. Twice a year, in June, and December, coupons will be drawn 'from the hat' and the winner will receive a complete year's set of TARGET books.

Write to:

TARGET BOOKS
44 Hill Street
London W1X 8LB

cut here

Full name ....

Address..

....

....

Age......................

PLEASE ENCLOSE A SELF-ADDRESSED STAMPED ENVELOPE WITH YOUR COUPON!